BOY
IN THE
TREETOPS

BY DR. SAM NEWSOME

Published in 2021

by DW Beam Publishing

King, NC

Published in the USA in 2021

by DW Beam Publishing,
King, NC

http://www.dwbeampublishing.com

ISBN: 978-1-943455-34-8

Front Cover Art & Illustrations by Erica White
Back Cover Map courtesy of https://web.lib.unc.edu/nc-maps

PROLOGUE

"Ouch!"

"Callie, quit making such a fuss. You knew that you needed to keep that sunscreen applied. We've been at the beach ten days now, and you've done well till today."

"But it's so hot. I had to keep getting back in the water to cool off."

The Edwards family had been enjoying a long-overdue vacation to Myrtle Beach, South Carolina. The kids, Callie and Jeffy, had spent every day in the water, but after ten days of water, beach, sun, and sand, it was time for a break.

"Well, you know your father expects tomorrow to be his day, and it won't hurt you and Jeffy one bit to humor him while he does his thing."

The "thing" Madge Edwards was referring to was Chad Edwards' fascination with history. He had planned their beach vacation with the intention of attending a reenactment presented by a local college. This was a bit different from the Civil War or Revolutionary War battle reenactments that were prominent near major battlefields. This was termed a Plantation Day. One of the remaining antebellum plantations was to be the scene of a living reenactment of a typical day on a plantation. Mr. Edwards explained to his family that this was not an amusement park event or an exciting diversion. It was an opportunity to look at the plantation system with warts and all. He had looked forward to the event for months. His family was visibly less enthusiastic.

Madge again voiced her long-standing concern. "Plantation Day will be all about slavery, won't it? That's such a sensitive topic. Do you really want our children exposed to a reenactment of such a dark time?"

Chad had considered this very question and was ready with an answer. "Slavery was definitely a dark and complex part of our history, but it is *our* history. The people who designed Plantation Day are mostly descendants of slaves rather than slave owners. They realize that there were many aspects of slavery and plantation life, and the topic frequently seems to be seen from only one view by either side. Plantation day is controversial and has taken years of planning and negotiation to bring to reality. We had better go tomorrow. I don't know if there will ever be another such presentation. If there are any protestors at the plantation, we'll drive on by."

....

The family—Chad, Madge, Jeff, and Callie—arrived midmorning at the Hiatt plantation just south of Georgetown on the Santee River. Chad had talked positively about the experience. The children were indulging their father but were bored even as they exited Highway 17. Fortunately, the protesters that Madge feared never materialized.

Chad had seen pictures of the plantation house before. It was a large, stately house overlooking the Santee River with broad, manicured lawns. As their car negotiated the tree-lined lane to the estate, he could see immediately that care had been taken to preserve the historic ambience.

Instead of an evenly manicured lawn that had been pruned by gasoline-powered mowers and trimmers, they found sheep and cows grazing in the front lawn. Several black youths dressed in period costumes, including straw hats, homespun clothes, and bare feet, were tending the livestock to keep them in the boundaries of the lawn. The animals effectively sheared the grass, but their grazing didn't leave the homogenous effect of a modern groomed lawn.

4

After the family bought tickets at a kiosk, they were introduced to Amos, a handsome African American teenager who stated that he would be their guide for the day. He was lean and fit. He wore a broad-brimmed straw hat and a coarsely woven loose-fitting shirt absent of buttons. His patched pants were of a coarse and well-worn material, and they ended at midcalf with frayed cuffs. He was barefoot.

"I'll be takin' you to our kitchen house yonder way. Please follow me."

As he led the Edwards family on a path around the front lawn, Amos commented that the "massa" lived in the big house with his family. He commented that the inland side of the main house was actually the backside, and the riverside was considered the front and had featured a grander facade in the eighteenth and nineteenth centuries. As they rounded the side of the house, they saw a pier reaching out over the river. Callie noticed two young black boys who were perhaps nine or ten years old sitting on the end of the pier with their cane fishing poles in hand.

They arrived at a small-whitewashed building. Even though it was a hot mid-August day, there was a plume of smoke rising from the chimney. Amos stood aside and announced that here they would meet Aunt Bessie.

Aunt Bessie came to the door. Her voluminous dress was made of the same course material as Amos' shirt. She was a large woman, and with her loose skirts, she filled the doorway of the small frame building. Sweat beaded her forehead and stained her clothing. Although she was definitely not a young person like the others the Edwards had seen, they were unable to guess her age. Obviously, she would be the one outlining the activities for the visit.

"Thank y'all for visitin' the turn of the eighteenth century. We been waitin' fo' you to visit nigh on two hundred years. We take good care o' the rice and used to send indigo dye to that Mr. King George 'cross the sea. But after some unpleasant time, we don't make that dye no more. We just make the rice. This is the big-house kitchen. You see, we can't have a kitchen burn down and burn the house, so it's built a piece away from the fancy house. My folks eat from cookin' done on the fireplace in our little cabin or outdoors." Under her breath she said, "I think it tastes better than the regular kitchen food."

Bessie continued, "You folks will see the working plantation. Amos will show you the barns, the livestock, the rice fields, and the trunks—them's sluices that flood the rice fields. He'll show how the canals were made by our labor—meaning the labor of those held in slavery. Of course, you'll see the massa's house and all his fancy things. I'll wager that you folks will learn mo' 'bout the Hiatts and their lives here two hundred years ago than you ever thought possible. You'll learn 'bout the rice growin' and us who kept the Hiatts up.

Finally, Amos will bring you back to our part of the plantation, where we live, love, work, and suffer. You'll see our quarters, and I hope you come to understand the effort it took to maintain the plantation system, the system that did, with all its pain and problems, birth a nation. Do y'all have questions for Aunt Bessie?"

Callie raised her hand just as she would in school.

"Child, you go ahead and ask."

"We heard in school about how bad slavery was, but I see kids fishing and no one suffering. Was it bad or not?"

The big woman might have been jovial at first, but now she had a steely glint in her eyes that sent a chill down Callie's back.

"Child, you're just a baby. How would you feel if your daddy didn't come home one night? He didn't come home, and your mommy has to tell you that he done been sold to another plantation that now owns him and you won't never see him again. And what's mo', he would as likely as not be made to marry another woman without ever divorcing your ma, and he would likely have children by his new family. Now does that sound bad to you?"

Callie felt like crawling under a rock, but Bessie lightened up a bit.

"That does happen. In some plantations with hundreds of enslaved people, it happens often. The Hiatts, they's good folks. They don't sell no families. And Miss, she sees we get a pair of shoes every year. And we get a field dress every winter, and sometimes we gets handoffs from the family. And Massa Hiatt, he ain't bought no slaves in years. He puts on a good face, and he sure spoils his children, but we see them bankers comin' round. The plantation owners, they got their own owners. They as bound to the dirt of this land as we slaves is. They got them some land, they got a big ol' house, and man oh man, they put on a good front, but they ain't got much money. At least they ain't got enough to keep them bankers happy. Now little miss, do you read the Bible?"

"Yes, ma'am, and we go to church most Sundays."

"You ever read about slaves in the Bible? Now we slaves, we don't read. It's not allowed. We don't write neither. It's against the law to have pen or paper. A slave gets whupped iffen he's found with paper unless it's a permit from his massa. But slaves, they sure is there, they's all over the old and new parts of the Good Book. Now us slaves, hardly a one can read or write, but we sometimes goes to the white church, and they let us listen or even do us slaves a separate meetin'.

That man Paul, he preached about how them slaves should behave way back then. He wrote a letter to a massa called Philemon. This runaway slave, Onesimus, had been serving that good man, Paul. Onesimus wanted to go back to Massa Philemon. That man Paul wrote a letter and said that Massa Philemon should be a kind massa and should accept Mr. Onesimus as a brother, a brother in Christ.

And I'll tell you somethin' else, little missy. You people in the twenty-first century two hundred years from now, you're still slaves. You may not have a massa like Hiatt, but you got yo' own massas. You got a mortgage. You got a job to pay yo' bills. Yo' hooked to yo' gadgets and yo' credit card and yo' fancy-dancy lifestyle. You got yo' own master right there. Now ain't that so?

Now why don't we look all sad? Why don't we rise up? Why don't we just all dig a hole and go ahead and crawl in? 'Cause we done learned from our pappy and he learned from his pappy that this is our life. This is the only life we likely to have. Sometime, someday, our children or their children will make their own way, but in the meantime, we just got to endure. That's what we does —we endure. And while we endure, we find a little joy. That may be the greatest gift of our people. We find joy in living, in breathing. And in those times the fields don't need us, we take our ease, not for long and not often, but we make the best of them."

Chad and Marge were enjoying the give-and-take between Aunt Bessie and Callie. But they knew something about Bessie that Callie didn't. Bessie was really Dr. Millicent Anders. She had double doctorates in English and philosophy. The Plantation Day was the fruition of a project she had espoused for years. The enactors were mostly current and past students who had been carefully instructed and led in rehearsals on the plantation life of 1800.

Now Jeffy had a question. "I see dirt and pebble paths all around, but between the kitchen and the main house, I see this brick path. Why is that?"

Bessie looked at Jeffy with mild surprise. The youngsters who came to Plantation Day were usually too involved with their cell phones to observe the layout of the grounds.

"Well, child, that is a good question. On each side of that walk is what you would call a kitchen garden. It's close so we can get fresh vegetables, but more importantly, it produces fresh herbs for seasoning. The brick path is to get the food up to the main house real quick and free of dirt and dust 'fore it gets cold."

"They come out to get their food?"

"Lawd no! One of our children who is too small for field work gets dressed up in knee britches and carries the food up to Massa and Miss."

"Does he ever sneak a taste?"

"Well, no, he can't sneak no biscuit, 'cause he gots to whistle."

"Whistle?"

"Yes, whistle. That's one of the rules. He has to be able to whistle, or he can't be no houseboy. He whistles, and the massa's mouth starts watering 'cause he knows his food is comin'. And he whistles so the massa knows the boy ain't tastin' none o' his biscuits and gravy. Then when he gets there, after the housemaid dishes the food out, if it's summer, he grabs a big fan to shoo the flies away so the family can eat. He eats later."

Jeffy persisted, "Doesn't he ever get a taste?"

Aunt Bessie thought a minute, and as she thought, she seemed to look past Jeffy and the Edwards family and up into the dining-room windows of the big house, just as though she really was on the plantation grounds in 1800.

After a hesitation, she collected herself and answered, "Well, I've heard there was a time…"

CHAPTER ONE

The year was 1812, but plantation life depended more on seasons and weather than year. The sun winked over the Santee River, signaling the dawn of yet another plantation day. Mist swirled above the reeds in the marsh as the population of the Hiatt plantation shook off the last of their sleep and began to stir. Although the massa's household was still an hour from arising, the small village one hundred yards west known as The Quarter was already buzzing with activity. Among the row of small, neat-whitewashed cabins was the home of Sammy's multigenerational family. Inside the cabin there were two rooms with a bare planked floor and a fireplace. Sammy lived here with his momma, Big Annie who was the cook for the main house, his four older brothers and sisters, two uncles, and an aunt.

Sammy's momma was not in the cabin. She had risen early with the first crow of the cock. She had stoked the hot coals of their fireplace and put a pot of water on a hook over the fire to boil for a breakfast of mush. Then she had gone to the plantation kitchen to stoke another fire and start the breakfast for the massa.

Sammy rubbed sleep from his eyes and remembered that today was special for him. As his brothers and sisters shucked off their nightshirts and dressed in their field clothes, Sammy washed his face from the bucket in the corner and went off to the kitchen. He still wore his nightshirt, as Momma had instructed, and he remained barefoot like all the children, since shoes were only for older family members.

Momma was busy with kitchen duties and was moving quickly among the delicious smells surrounding the small white building with hickory-scented smoke rising from an enormous chimney. When she saw Sammy, she stopped long enough to give him a pat on the head and a smile. "This is yo' special day. You get washed up, and I'll fix you some grits and milk, and I may even be able to find a slice of fatback."

Sammy remembered that his momma had said today would be special, but he didn't think his eleventh birthday was until the fall, after the frost. Then he remembered that Momma had told him he would be special because he could avoid the fields.

"Have you been practicin'?"

"Yes'm. I been puckerin' up and puttin' my tongue way up behind my top teeth."

His momma knew he had practiced because she had heard it most of the day recently. Sammy loved to climb. The slave street was partially sheltered from the hot Carolina sun by tall pine trees. Sammy's favorite pastime was climbing the trees. He would go to the very top of trees over one hundred feet tall. Sometimes he could be seen riding a treetop as it bent back and forth in the wind. From this viewpoint, he could feel the wind in his hair and get a sight of the sea that he had never visited. That was where he had practiced his whistle.

Momma had heard him whistling and would look up in the treetops. He was so high she could barely see him. She should have been worried, but what else was a young enslaved boy to do? His future was backbreaking work in a rice field that would inevitably lead to an early death, so if he got some joy from climbing, she wouldn't stop him. His time for climbing would be short now anyhow.

"Well, now, you whistle loud and make a tune iffen you can."

Noon came, and Annie helped Sammy into a frilly white shirt and stiff, itchy knee britches. His stockings reached all the way up to the knee britches, and he had shiny black leather shoes with big brass buckles. He had never worn stockings before and had only rarely worn his brother's or his uncle's plantation-made shoes with wooden soles. He had a waistcoat and a tricornered hat to complete his livery.

When one o'clock came, Annie placed a wooden yoke on Sammy's shoulders and attached a white oak basket to each end of the yoke. The burden was not heavy. It was lighter than the firewood he helped keep supplied for the cabin's fireplace.

Sammy began the walk up the brick path to the main house. The britches itched, and the shoes were too large and flapped up and down on his feet. When he heard his momma say from behind, "Don't you forget to whistle," he began whistling. He really didn't know any tunes, but his whistling may have eventually sounded like "Go Down Moses." The smell of the hot biscuits, country ham, and sweet potatoes made his mouth water and his stomach growl, but he whistled as loud as possible, even as he developed spittle running down his chin.

It took only a few minutes to reach the house, and the housemaid came to the door to unload his burden.

The housemaid took the food to a warming room. Ordinarily, the food had to be rewarmed there and lost some of its initial flavor and fresh texture. The biscuits would seem doughy, rather than fresh and fluffy. But she discovered that the food was just the right temperature and no repeat warming was needed. She immediately took the prepared meal to the family, who were already impatient for their dinner. She led Sammy into the dining room and directed him to stand in the corner before announcing his presence.

"Massa, this here's little Sammy. He's Cook Annie's young'un. He's her youngest, and I reckon she's dried up, so she won't have no mo'. He's pretty much the runt of the litter, so he's not likely to be much of a field hand yet. But he's near perfect for a kitchen boy to see yo' meals is hot."

Massa Hiatt considered this for a few moments. He scraped his chair away from the table before he stood up, so that his large belly would not disrupt the whole table. "Well, he's not much bigger than a June bug. He does dress up nice in that finery. He looks like a real little dandy. Why, I guess he'll pass. I think he'll do right well. You say his name is Sammy?'

"Yessir, Sammy Hiatt."

"I may call you Sammy, but Sambo seems to fit better. Yep, Sambo does pretty well, and I guess you'll do."

Sammy was perplexed. He didn't want to be the runt of the litter, but he was glad the massa was pleased with him, and he was even happier that he wouldn't have as much time in the field. He was given a large fan woven from a palm frond and was told to keep fanning, to keep the flies off the family and their food.

After the family's meal was complete, they retired to another part of the house, and Sammy's baskets were again placed over his shoulders for return to the kitchen. They were not nearly as heavy now, and the maid told him there was no need to whistle on the return walk.

Momma was pleased when she heard that the family was happy with her son. Sammy was happy that after he got his fine, uncomfortable clothes off and put away, he was able to eat the leftovers. He had passed his audition, and for a while, he would be better fed than his brothers and sisters, and he could, for the most part, avoid the hardships of long hours in the fields.

As the spring planting progressed and the weather warmed, Sammy continued his daily whistling walk to the massa's house. He grew tired of the frequent baths required to keep his clothes clean, and he felt like the family was using him as decoration, but it was still better than the grueling South Carolina sun burning down on the fields.

CHAPTER TWO

Sammy continued to deliver hot food to the massa once or twice a day. He was sometimes put on display and ordered to whistle a tune for guests. As the days got warmer, the spring rains swelled the river, and the rice was flooded for the first time of the year. Sammy was excited to see a ship approaching up the Santee. The great ship was the grandest thing Sammy had ever seen. It was much larger than the boats that occasionally visited the plantation. In truth, he had never seen much. He had never been off the plantation.

The ship was tied up at the pier near the main house. The crew lowered the sails and began to unload cargo, which consisted mostly of things that couldn't be produced by the plantation or bartered for locally. Bolts of fine cloth for the family, stores such as coffee, and spices for food preparation were important. There was a fine French clock and other treasures to make low-country life more bearable for the plantation owners. Panes of glass, metal implements, and all sorts of finery unavailable at the plantation were unloaded. Massa Hiatt and his family came down to the river in their finest clothes to greet the visitors.

Finally, the ship's captain stepped down the gangplank and onto the pier. He was a portly man with olive skin that suggested he was of Latin origin. Rather than the traditional captain's garb of a seafarer, he was dressed in a plain shirt and a straw hat. He held his right arm high, holding the handle of a package. It was covered with a linen cloth.

Massa greeted him with great enthusiasm. "Ah, Captain Mendoza, I see you have something for me."

"And I am glad to see you again, Señor Hiatt. It wasn't easy, but I have found a magnificent specimen for you. The Brits, they make it difficult to trade. They care not whether we're American or Spanish. They'll take our sailors onto their ships all the same. President Madison needs to protect our ships 'cause on the sea, it's every sailor for himself. I can smell the scent of a new war in the air—and soon."

Hiatt looked over Mendoza's vessel and remarked, "Your ship seems to be well defended. Since your last visit to Georgetown you've added some armament."

"Aye, I have to defend myself, and I will defend my crew, my ship, and my cargo." Then he leaned closer to Massa and in a conspiratorial whisper said, "And there may be an opportunity for a small profit."

They proceeded to the main house, where beverages and other refreshments were served prior to dinner. Sammy was summoned to dress up and stand in the corner of the room, fanning to provide some breeze and freedom from the flies and mosquitoes.

After the initial pleasantries were exchanged, Massa Hiatt prodded Captain Mendoza to reveal the specimen. With great fanfare, the captain removed the cover from the item he had carried from the ship, revealing a cage fashioned out of bamboo. In the cage was a large red and green bird with a yellow tail. Mendoza said it was a macaw, a type of parrot.

Hiatt was amazed at the sight of the bird. "What does he say? How many words does it speak?"

"Señor, this is a healthy specimen and no doubt will be talking as soon as you teach it to speak. They don't speak naturally in the jungle. They don't have conversations with the bird in the next tree. And I doubt that they know what they say, except I hear they respond to food. Start training it. Give it a reward of some fruit or other food when it does speak, and soon it will be talking like a drunken sailor. Now, Señor Hiatt, what is the story behind the bambino standing in the corner?"

"That's just a servant boy. He's the son of our cook and too frail for the fields, so he dresses up our place. He sees that the food gets up here from the kitchen house while it's still warm and keeps the flies out of the house. My wife likes to see him dressed up. It makes her feel like royalty."

Sammy didn't hear all that they said, but it felt odd that they were speaking of him like he wasn't even there.

CHAPTER THREE

Life on the plantation was severe. The field hands worked whenever the sun and the weather allowed, and food was truly at the mercy of the elements. Almost everything they ate was grown or hunted on the plantation.

The work was allotted on a "task" system. A fit adult was expected to complete a task in nine hours. A child such as Sammy's older brother, Johnny, would be assigned a half task. If a task could not be completed, there was always the possibility of punishment. There were times when the kitchen gardens were plentiful, and the staples supplied made life easier. And there were times on the plantation when even those who were enslaved had some time to themselves. The adults who completed a task early had time to work their private gardens, especially during those long summer days. The children who had begun to work in the fields would play a little but would also fish and try to catch some game to supplement their diet.

Johnny, Sammy's older and stronger brother, had a love of all wild animals. He spent his spare moments communing with the wildlife in the area. He had a pet king snake that he kept in his pocket. He would pull the snake from his pocket and allow it to crawl over and under his fingers. It would slither down the neck of his nightshirt and then appear at the tail of his shirt, having wriggled down his body, along his chest, abdomen, and thighs.

Massa Hiatt became enamored with his parrot. He put the parrot on a perch in the sitting room and spent hours training the parrot to speak. Miss Hiatt called him an old fool for spending so much time trying to get that dumb bird to mimic speech, but Massa wouldn't give up.

The bird sat on the perch and ate crackers, crusts, fruit, and crumbs, but all he verbalized were screeches and chirps; no words poured from his beak.

Massa was not a patient man at his best, and instead of this experience soothing his temper as Miss had hoped, Massa seemed to become more agitated when he was training the parrot.

The family usually summered in Charleston or Georgetown to escape the heat and swamp fever, but this year, Hiatt decided to forego the expensive summer at the seaside. Miss could tell that the family was in trouble. The bankers were visiting and threatening constantly. Plantations in the area were owned as much by the banks as by the planters. He could sell some slaves to ease the financial burden, but he had pledged to Miss not to, and he still had to grow rice and a little cotton to be profitable. Rather than trade slaves and break up families, he would try to be more productive.

As the summer continued, the windows were flung wide open more during the day to allow some relief from the severe heat. And to top all of Massa Hiatt's other troubles, he still couldn't make his parrot talk. It seemed that the only thing Massa took pleasure in was hearing the now-familiar whistle of Sammy walking up the brick pathway to the house. He had continued calling him Sambo.

Every evening following dinner, Massa Hiatt spent a couple of hours coaxing the parrot to speak, always with the same lack of success. This time, the stress of the day and the failure with the parrot was so severe that Massa Hiatt picked up a book from the library table and threw it at the bird. The book missed, but the bird had at some point slipped its leg leash, and now it flew through the open window. Hiatt was so enraged that he went to his gun cabinet and swore to shoot the bird and have Cook Annie stew it.

The bird circled the main house and finally lit high in the branches of a tall pine tree behind the kitchen. Hiatt charged his flintlock and was ready to fire at the bird, but the animal seemed to know Hiatt was looking and stayed out of sight whenever Hiatt appeared. Finally, he gave up, but he swore he would get rid of the defective bird.

Over the next weeks, the bird would make occasional appearances that only seemed to infuriate Massa Hiatt. On more than one occasion, he took his old scattershot blunderbuss and attempted to hit the parrot. He might have eventually gotten lucky with the ancient gun, but when the scattered shot began hitting the roofs in the slave quarter, Miss put an end to that.

CHAPTER FOUR

Seasons passed and plantation life continued. In a society without the constant barrage of information from radios or television, life passed at a more relaxed pace. The rare newspapers didn't matter to a population that was mostly illiterate.

Sammy continued his house duties and became accepted as one of the family's personal servants. He would stand in the corner, slowly waving his fan as the family carried on their meal conversations. Massa always surveyed the fare and said a short grace being thankful for the food and the land that produced it. After the blessing, the housemaid would see that everyone was served. The children always were fickle eaters and intent on avoiding foods they didn't like. Sammy couldn't understand their reluctance to eat, as he always seemed to be hungry. The girl, Emily, was a bit younger and smaller than Sammy. She would push the food around on her plate and occasionally pretend to feed her dolly or the old hound slouching beneath the table. The boy, Francis, was slightly larger than Sammy, but he had heard that they were almost the same age. Francis had pale skin and a freckled face. He favored his father, Massa Hiatt.

Massa was talking about some visitors that were expected in the next few days. "Now you children, try to behave. We need to impress these Georgetown bankers so they see what a good investment we are."

Francis piped in, "What's so special about these visitors?"

Massa became serious, "These are the men who have a great deal of influence. They have a majority interest in a several plantations including this one."

Miss cut Massa short. "Now don't you be troubling the children with so much of your business matters. The children are growing up much too fast as it is. They don't need to worry about plantation problems, at least not yet."

Massa changed to a discussion of the quality of the vittles, and began gazing out the window toward The Quarter trying to spy that pesky bird.

Back in the kitchen, Sammy told his momma, Big Annie, some of what he had heard. "Lawd Sammy, you best forget all that. What you hear at the big house, stays there. Don't you be tellin' anybody anything you hear. That ain't nothing but trouble."

....

That early March afternoon was unexpectedly warm. Sammy's brother, Johnny, had completed his task early as usual and was in the mood to fish. The boys were sitting on the wharf by The Quarter, half dozing and half fishing. Sammy was playing with a gadget his uncle had made for him. The boys had landed a few fish, enough to add to momma's stew. Sammy's toy was very common among the children of The Quarter. It consisted of a large button; it was fully two inches across and too large for clothing with two small holes in the center. String was threaded through the holes and attached to a small wooden handle on each side. Sammy would sling the button between the handles till the string was thoroughly twisted and then make a pulling and slacking motion with his hands on the handles. The resulting sound was like the wind filling sails on a boat. The button jumped as though it was one of Johnny's critters. Watching the button spin first in one direction and then reverse was hypnotic. It was a good way to pass the time between nibbles from the fish. Sammy was surprised to hear steps on the creaky boards of the wharf.

"Whatcha doin' there?" Sammy awoke enough to look around and see Francis walking out over the water. The Massa's son was carrying his own fishing pole and small basket of dirt that was moving with the wiggle of worms. "Can I put a hook in the water with you?"

Aside from his pale, freckled complexion, Francis didn't look much different from Sammy or Johnny. His pants were of the same coarse weave as the boys' and his shirt had the same homespun pattern though his clothes were obviously less worn and less patched. His straw hat was identical and all three were barefoot.

Soon hooks were re-loaded and again in the water. The boys sat waiting a strike of a big fish. Francis enjoyed the time spent with Johnny and Sammy. Most of the other slave children were different ages, and he enjoyed the company of children nearly his own age. Momma had cautioned the boys about being too familiar with the "Family," but they were just boys playing regardless of class or status.

Johnny asked, "I thought you had to spend today riding around the fields with your pa. How come you come down here with us?"

Francis answered, "Pa got company. Those fancy men in tall hats came up the river and pa had to meet them. I think he's afeared of them."

Sammy again began the rhythmic motion of his new toy. As the button twirled away, Sammy began to make a rhyme.

"Francis, Francis, where you been?
'Round the bend and back again.
Francis, Francis where you goin'?
Gonna catch his fish and take it home.
He gonna have our ma cook it in a pot.
She gonna make fish stew to feed a lot."

22

All three boys laughed at Sammy's made up verse. Sammy asked a question he had been curious about for some time. "Francis, how'd you get that funny name? We don' know no other Francis, neither boy nor girl."

Francis thought for a moment before answering. "I didn't like my name for a long time. Emily thought I was a girl. Then my pa told me that I was named after a great hero, Colonel Francis Marion, the Swamp Fox. Pa says he was the bravest and smartest patriot of the war." The boys had heard of the war, but had little interest. "Colonel Marion had them British running around in circles so bad that they were chasing their own tails."

Now it was Francis' turn. "Who are you named after?"

Johnny had an answer. "Well I reckon I'm named after you. I'm Johnny Hiatt and this here's Sammy Hiatt."

All three boys laughed. The complicated truth of one person owning another and sharing a name did not at that moment matter.

"What is that thing you got there?" Francis asked while pointing at Sammy's toy.

That's somethin' Uncle Jap made. He calls it a *Whimmidittle*."

The whirling continually humming button fascinated Francis. "Will he make me one?"

"I'll ask him. I reckon he might. It just takes a sharp knife and a little string."

....

Back in the main house, Hiatt was prepared to host his uninvited guests. He had expected their visit even though in the low country of South Carolina time had its own rhythm. He had prepared refreshments for his guests, but had a queezy feeling in his bowels as their boat was tied to the pier. The three bankers hurried up the hill to the main house without a look at the plantation grounds or the rice fields or the livestock. They were a curious looking trio. The first off the boat was a tall thin fellow. He seemed to be more agile than the others and walked with a long stride and his head held high and his nose at a distinctly upward angle that signified his superiority over the country folks. The second off the boat was a short rotund man in his later years. He appeared to have spent very little time outside. He awkwardly stepped off the boat, nearly stumbling. His coat was straining at the buttons and he had a fringe of reddish-gray hair. Beneath the edges of his hat a bald head could be seen. The third man was dressed in the manner of a low country laborer and was likely a caretaker for the other two. He carried ledger books tucked under his arm. They made a beeline to the house as though they wore blinders. They had no interest in the daily activities of the plantation. The unusually warm spring afternoon had little effect on the creditors who wore their waistcoats and top hats as though they were on the waterfront of Georgetown rather than a working plantation on an unseasonably warm March afternoon.

Hiatt greeted them with warm handshakes and greetings he didn't really feel. He offered them cooled glasses of cider and they did enjoy the libation, but Hiatt could tell that they were eager to get their business done and take their leave.

As Hiatt passed the window overlooking The Quarter, he could not help but glance at the tall pines to see if he saw the bird. He thought he had a glimpse of a red patch high up a waving pine top and would have reached for his weapon if his guests had not immediately behind him entering his library.

The taller and seemingly superior of the three seemed to be the spokesman. He opened and laid the books on the large table in the middle of the library. "Here are the books of the Hiatt plantation. This first one is the assets of the Hiatt land including buildings, timber, acreage, and chattel (chattel included livestock, harvested crops and of course, your work force)." He didn't use the word 'slave' but that was understood.

"This next book recorded the income generated by the property over the last ten years." The tall slender banker turned the pages slowly as though they were sacred texts. He ran his index finger along the bottom line of each page and emphasized the rather stagnate income generated by the plantation. The thin man said with an air of authority, "as you can see, the value of the property has gradually increased, but the income generated by your operation has not improved in a similar fashion."

Hiatt was familiar with the figures and tried to make an explanation. "Rice cultivation is not like being a storekeeper. We have to deal with weather, our workforce and demand of the rice market. In a good year we make a profit, and in a worse year we have to survive till times improve."

The shortest of the three; the elderly bald fellow with a fringe of red hair that fell down over his collar stepped to the table and said in a nasal voice that also reflected an air of superiority. "Our investment in the Hiatt plantation is not charity. The bank can't be influenced by bad years or the rumor that you coddle both your animals and your workforce. We need to see tangible evidence of profits, and that brings us to our third ledger."

This ledger was thinner and Hiatt felt it was the most menacing of all. This ledger was a record of money owed to the bank. In Hiatt's case it was money owed to several banks. The baldy reported. "Your operation here has been tettering on the brink of insolvency for years. We have carried you for years and its time that some changes are made."

Hiatt knew his condition was tenuous and with a frail voice responded. "I'm willing to do anything reasonable to save our plantation."

The thin man pointed to the first ledger. "Here is a big part of the problem. Your workforce is much too large. You should be getting more production out of your slaves, or you can get rid of some. You are taking care of families where there are few productive workers and you have several that are just too old to work. You need to cull the weak and inefficient from the herd." He pointed to the third more plainly clothed man. "This is Roger Evans. Roger is in the business of making your work force, Uh, slave force, more efficient. He may be able to make this ledger more favorable."

Hiatt interrupted. "You mean he's a slave trader."

The red headed man responded. "He is a number of things, but, yes, he does handle such arrangements."

Hiatt had expected he would hear such a statement, but it still came as a shock. Again, he stuttered as he responded. "These are families that have only known this plantation as their home. I've promised Miss that I would keep the families together. They know more about rice cultivation than I ever will. We'll just have to be more efficient and pray for a bountiful harvest."

The small man retorted. "Times change and plantations change. Perhaps it's time you took your family to Georgetown and left the plantation. This land is unhealthy for most of the year anyhow."

Hiatt had been fully cowed. "We'll just have to do better, be more efficient and plant more rice."

Again, the elder of the group made a statement. "We fear that your time here is limited and we may need to put this land into the hands of someone who understands the economics of the rice plantation better than you." As he said this, he nodded to the third fellow that had previously been identified as a slave trader. "We don't need a social experiment; we need a planter who understands economics. Why, you could greatly reduce your debt by selling just ten percent of your most unproductive units."

Hiatt responded. "If you mean selling people or families. That is not possible. It's not something I can do."

"Perhaps you could sell just part of families rather than whole units."

Hiatt could see that a noncommittal answer would be his only course. "I will consider any reasonable action to retain our plantation."

The retort from the shorter man was terse and clear. "You may, after all, be more suited to a retail job along the waterfront of Georgetown rather than the backwoods along the swampy banks of the Santee."

The trio from Georgetown did not stay for a meal even though Big Annie had prepared them a feast. They were escorted to their boat where boatmen from the town had been waiting and hustled them back on board. They were soon in the channel where the current propelled them back faster than they came. Hiatt was relieved to see them go, but he knew that they would be back.

CHAPTER FIVE

Sammy was now called Sambo so often by the massa that he answered to that as easily as Sammy. He had become a regular in the main house, and the family seemed to accept his presence as they would that of any servant or even a favorite pet.

But Sammy was changing. The summer months had seen a growth spurt, and as the fall approached, his body was changing. He would soon be eleven, and he had noticed a little dark shadow above his lip and that his voice sometimes cracked when he spoke. His momma had let out his waistcoat and britches twice, but his once-floppy shoes now were starting to pinch his toes when he walked.

Momma seemed concerned and frowned at these changes. "My, my, you sure are gettin' to be a big boy. But don't you let the family hear you talk too much. And let's see if we can scrape a little of that peach fuzz from your lip." She was concerned that when the massa saw that Sammy was maturing, the boy would be turned out of the house and sent back to fieldwork.

Sammy noticed that the food he was given by his momma was no longer meeting the needs of a growing boy. His hunger was never satisfied. And his grumbling stomach seemed to get louder and louder as he carried vittles up to the main house. One thing he noted was that his whistling was more proficient. Not only was his whistling loud enough that the family could easily hear it through a closed window, but he could also carry a tune.

That was a good thing, since he sometimes wondered if his hunger pains could be heard over the whistling.

One afternoon, Sammy was delivering the afternoon dinner meal to the family when he began hearing an echo of his whistle. Several days passed, and the echo of his whistle recurred. Curiously, the only time he heard the echo was when he was delivering the massa's food on the brick pathway.

Everyone on the plantation was aware of the massa's consternation with the colorful bird. It was now regarded as a regular, though unwelcome, visitor to the pines shading the slave quarters. One afternoon, Sammy began his walk up the brick pathway and quit after a few whistled breaths. He heard "Go Down Moses" continue even after he quit. Looking around, he saw the bird high up in a tree, closely mimicking his whistled sound. It even was passably carrying the tune. Sammy didn't whistle the rest of the way to the main house, and there was no comment from Massa Hiatt indicating that he had noticed anything different.

When Sammy arrived back at the kitchen, his momma was sobbing. She was weeping more than Sammy had ever seen. "Momma, what's wrong?"

"It's Johnny, yo' brother li'l Johnny. He's gone."

"Momma, where's he gone?"

"Jesus took him, honey. Took him off to heaven just like Elijah in a fiery chariot!"

"Will he be back?"

Momma sat him down and hugged him while she spoke through her tears. "You know Johnny loved everythin' that lived and breathed. He 'specially liked them critters that others don't want. I've warned him about them snakes before—there's so many that ain't as harmless as you think. You know we talked about those coral snakes. I tol' him how *red on black is all right, Jack, but red on yellow will kill a fella!* He was out in the rice field and just picked up a coral snake like it was a colorful little wiggly thing. I can see why 'cause it is right pretty, but it killed him. It killed my li'l Johnny so quick he couldn't even say goodbye."

29

As Momma said this, she held Sammy close and rocked him back and forth. She held him so tight that he thought she would smother him in her ample breasts.

Through her sobs, she remarked, "I'm not going to let you go to the fields. They took Johnny, and I won't let them take you."

Sammy couldn't believe Johnny was gone. They had spent every night curled up together on a straw tick by the fireplace, entwined so closely that it was impossible to tell where Sammy stopped and Johnny started. Now Johnny would never be there to share a straw tick again. One thing Sammy knew for certain was that Momma was right: he could not go to the fields to work. Johnny had always been the stronger of the two boys, and if the fields had killed him, then Sammy didn't have a chance. If he had to spend his life as a 'houseboy,' he would do so, but going to the fields would be the end of him.

CHAPTER SIX

Grief could be a terrible thing. Sometimes it knocked everything else out of your head. Sammy was so overcome with grief for his closest friend and brother that he forgot about everything else. But on the plantation, there was very little time for grief. Johnny was sewn into a shroud and nailed into a box. The box was covered in black pitch, as was the custom of the times. As was usual among slaves, he was buried at night. Aided by torches made from burning pine knots, a small group of Johnny's family made their way to the slave graveyard to lay Johnny to his final rest.

As they walked, the small procession sang a sweet, haunting song about another child who had undergone hardship.

Sweet little Jesus boy, they made you be born in a manger
Sweet little holy child, we didn't know who you was
Didn't know you'd come to save us, Lord,
To take our sins away
Our eyes were blind
We could not see. We didn't know who you was
You have shown us how we are trying
Master, you have shown us how, even when you were dying
It just seems like we can't do right
Look how we treated you, but please forgive us, Lord
We didn't know it was you
Sweet little Jesus boy, born long ago

Sweet little holy child
And we didn't know who you was

The mourners sang the song twice, and then they began softly humming the spiritual nativity song. Their humming eventually transformed into grievous wailing that was loud and from the heart. As Johnny's coffin was lowered, Annie had to be restrained to allow her son's burial to be completed. Finally, she held her remaining children fiercely and allowed the internment. The custom of the time among slaves was to have no grave marker or any other identification of the gravesite. Though mostly Christian, they still didn't want any evil spirits to disturb their dead. So Johnny's thin body would be lost to the ages and become part of the Carolina soil. Death was a final equalizer that eventually befell everything living.

Far away from the group of mourners, two small figures hid in the pines beside the path. They witnessed the ritual and wiped their own tears. Emily and Francis mourned the loss of Johnny privately. They had also lost a friend and were confused and saddened by the ritual that was so different from those they had witnessed in their own church.

The next morning, Annie's family resumed their duties as though it was a normal day. No doubt, Annie and her family had heavy hearts following Johnny's death, but the plantation system had no space for grief. Sammy once again made his way to the main house. He changed his tune to "Sweet Little Jesus Boy." That had been Johnny's favorite, which was part of why the mourners had sung it repeatedly as the procession accompanied Johnny to his final rest.

Sammy completed his duties as quickly as possible and went to the surrounding forest. In the forest, he was alone, so no one could see his tears. He didn't want Momma to see him crying. He cried his eyes dry. After some time, he wiped his swollen eyes with his long shirttail and looked about to be sure no one was witnessing his weakness. The only witness was the parrot. The colorful bird had taken a perch on a low branch rather than the safer, usually favored pine top. The bird's permanently wide eyes seemed to stare a hole through Sammy. He similarly stared at the parrot.

"Whatcha doin' up there?" Sammy said. "You feel bad too?"

The parrot turned his head almost totally around to his back. Then he began bobbing his head up and down in a pecking movement, though there was no food to be had.

"I won't have Johnny to talk to or to play or fish with no more. He won't be there with me on a pallet in front of the fireplace anymore. I'll never see him again."

The bird was silent, though he seemed to be listening. At least Sammy thought he was paying attention. After a pause, he added, "Well, I guess you got pulled away from your family too, Bird. I miss Johnny, but I'll bet you miss yo' ma and pa."

Then the inexplicable happened: the parrot flew into the clearing and alighted on Sammy's shoulder. Whether the bird shared Sammy's grief was questionable, but it made him feel better.

From that day, Sammy would look up into the tall pines before he began his daily walk to the main house. He continued to whistle the tunes of the old spirituals he had heard from infancy. "Go Down Moses" and "Swing Low, Sweet Chariot" were still his main tunes, and now he had added "Sweet Little Jesus Boy" since Johnny's funeral. But he had heard a new one from the adults, and he couldn't get it out of his head. Soon he added "Old Dan Tucker" to his repertoire.

Bird's mimicry continued. Sammy would whistle a few seconds of the tune, and the parrot would complete the song. One day, as Sammy began his walk, Bird began the song all on his own without any prompting. Over the next month, Bird whistled Sammy's tunes in a seemingly random fashion.

The day came that Sammy's feet were more sore than usual from the tight shoes, and his growing muscles were straining the seams of his britches and waistcoat. If that wasn't bad enough, his stomach was growling, and he was hungry beyond his endurance. His body was telling him that it needed more calories for his growth and activity. The smells of bacon and buttered biscuits from the baskets were maddening. He looked into the

33

windows of the main house and could see through the open windows that the family had not yet entered the dining room.

Sammy reached into the basket and felt for a biscuit. He didn't mean to, but before he could stop himself, he had begun to eat a biscuit. It took only a few seconds to polish off the delicious treat. It was so satisfying.

The housemaid received the baskets and was immediately suspicious. The cloth was not folded over the biscuits in Annie's normal careful fashion. The count was one short from the usual, and she noticed a drop of butter on Sammy's lip and some crumbs on his fancy shirt. "Well, you done it now. Massa will know fo' sure that you be stealin' his food."

"Don't tell. I swear, I won' do it no mo'." But down deep, Sammy knew he would. The temptation was just too great.

He took his fan, and standing in the corner, he fanned the family as usual to shoo away the flies. He had never made eye contact with any of the family unless directly spoken to. It had been an accepted custom in the past, but now he felt as though all the family was staring at him. Every time he waved the fan, he felt that Massa would look up and call him a thief.

Massa finally looked up and said, "Annie is shorting us on the biscuits." He looked around the room.

Sammy was certain he would be called out as a thief and flogged and then sold away from the plantation, the only home he had ever known.

Finally, after a too-long silence, Massa said, "She must think that I'm getting too fat. She may be right." Then he looked over at Sammy. "Sambo, you sure are growing. You'll be big enough to go to the field anytime now. Why, I'd think you were eating my house food, except we clearly heard your whistling. That was you whistling, wasn't it?"

As Sammy was stammering his answer, Massa Hiatt looked out the window toward the kitchen. There, high above the kitchen in the top of a tall pine, he saw that damned parrot.

Sammy felt his skin flush. He said, "I whistled as hard as I could." He didn't say that he had been unable to whistle with a mouth full of Massa's biscuit. Sammy knew at that moment that

34

he would be leaving the plantation. And his leaving would be soon.

After his duties were finished in the main house, he didn't go back to the kitchen house to change his clothing. Instead, he hid in the forest. He was ashamed of his inability to do his task and felt he had let his momma down. He put his head against a tall pine tree and cried till the tears would no longer flow. For the second time, Bird lit on his shoulder.

CHAPTER SEVEN

Momma heard from the housemaid that Sammy had admitted to eating a biscuit on the way to the main house. The housemaid had recounted the brief encounter with the massa. Momma was still reeling from the loss of one son. Now it seemed that her little Sammy was destined to go to the field. It had been inevitable that he would outgrow his current duties, but she doubted that the frail child could withstand the hardships of the fieldwork, which broke even strong men.

Even though the hot summer months were over, the weather was still unseasonably warm. The Hiatts had decided to spend the rest of the year in Charleston after all. The rumor was that the creditors would be taking over the plantation, and the Hiatts might not return even when the cooler weather came. But creditors or not, the heat around the plantation was unhealthy, hot, and simply unbearable. Swamp fever was a real threat that took people in the summer, but also in other seasons. So the Hiatts would soon be leaving to finish the year in Charleston where there were parties and more suitable weather. The flooded rice fields were necessary for the cultivation of rice, but they also brought the swamp fever. The family would be closer to the offshore breezes and away from the unrelenting heat of the plantation that seemed to persist long after the summer passed. They might return after Christmas, but the old-timers on the plantation suspected the Hiatts were done. Sammy knew that he wouldn't be around to see the first frost either. The fieldwork would kill him before then.

Before dark, Sammy returned home with his mind made. *I'm leavin'*, he told himself. *I've got to go. Massa don't want me in the house. He wants me in the field.*

Sammy knew his fate in the field would be the same as Johnny's. Johnny had been bigger and stronger and smarter than he. Sammy missed Johnny so much that if he couldn't be with Johnny, he would just leave. He went to the cabin, shucked off his fine outfit, and put on Johnny's field clothes.

In the kitchen, his momma was just cleaning up, and she was crying as she scrubbed the pots. She knew she was about to lose another child. "Are you gonna leave me? You are, ain't you?"

"Momma, I can't stay. I can't do what Johnny did, and I don't wanna be no houseboy no mo'."

"Well, I reckon yo' bound to leave. Now you be careful and watch them patrollers. They'll bring you back and whop you for a fare-thee-well."

The patrollers' job was to keep slaves from running away. A slave had to have written permission from his master or overseer to leave the plantation. Being caught by a patroller meant severe punishment. He would be severely flogged, and if he survived that, he might be sold.

"Where you gonna go?"

"I've got an idea, but I best not tell you. You'll be asked, and so better you not know."

Annie filled a sack with some biscuits and fatback and gave her youngest a long, smothering hug. It was a hug that would last the rest or their lives. Then she sent Sammy on his way.

....

The path down by the river was filled with gravel chips that hurt Sammy's feet. He wore Johnny's field clothes made of coarse homegrown fabrics. He had tried on Johnny's shoes, but they were so worn that going barefoot was easier.

The full moon made the path easier, but he still didn't know which way to go. Following the sunset would take him into the wilderness, and he had heard about Indians and wild animals. The strange ship that had visited and brought Bird fascinated him. The direction the ship had come from and left in was downstream, but in that direction, there would be more people. People would question why a little black boy was traveling alone.

The river shone in the moonlight. He walked the shoreline, feeling the squishy river mud between his toes, and occasionally waded into the edge of the water when the shoreline became impassable. He remembered his momma's stories of gators and how they would eat little boys who played too long at the edge of the water, but he had to put all that to the back of his mind. He kept a close watch on the moonlight-bathed water to see if there was any movement. He tried to listen closely for the swish of a gator tail or the rustle of the reeds at the water's edge that would indicate he wasn't alone. He also watched the shoreline and the banks for the patrollers. He half-thought that Momma would be coming to fetch him, but she did not make an appearance. The one place he forgot to look was the sky. He didn't notice a shadow passing immediately overhead in the light cast from the full moon.

CHAPTER EIGHT

Fatigue overcame Sammy when he felt he was far enough away from the plantation that he could not be found. He had no idea if he was still on plantation land or not because he had heard that Massa Hiatt's land extended almost to the big water.

His feet were sore and cut from the sharp edges of shells and reeds. His skin itched from the scratches of saw grass, and the mosquitoes and flies seemed to gather around him in a cloud. He walked inland from the river till he was on a slight rise above the water, in a wooded thicket. He thought he was far enough from the water that a gator wouldn't be tempted. Just to be safe, he found a live oak tree and climbed onto one of the low branches, made himself a little nest, and fell asleep. He was so tired from the day's activities and the weeks of grief over Johnny that he didn't even open the parcel Momma had made him.

Sammy awoke as the morning sun began to cast rays through the leaves and needles and onto his face. As his eyes fluttered open, he felt movement near his shoulder. He lay very still for fear that a snake had slithered up the tree and was ready to gobble him up, but to his surprise there was Bird. The animal was perched on a branch right by Sammy's shoulder and seemed to be reaching down at the boy's side to get something. Sammy realized it was his sack of food the bird was after.

"What are you doing here? I guess you and me both had just 'bout enough of Massa. They won't make you work in the field, but they may just have you fo' supper if you stay. So you wanna come with me?"

Bird seemed to nod his head yes, but it was a typical bird movement and could have meant anything or nothing. To Sammy, it was enough indication that he was not alone. He and Bird shared a biscuit, and the boy climbed down from the tree and headed back to the river. He didn't recognize anything familiar on the riverbank. He had gone farther down the river than he had ever been. He looked across to the other side of the river and saw a dead log floating in the water. It caught his attention, and as he watched more closely, he saw that the log was slowly moving. On even closer inspection, he saw that one end of the log had eyes. He counted himself lucky for having made it through the night and decided that he and Bird would risk moving in the daytime, but they would be on extra special watch for the dangers of the river—dangers from men and from animals.

Sammy and Bird moved carefully down the riverside. They reached one of the many irrigation canals for rice cultivation that originated in the Santee. Sammy crossed slowly and carefully, watching for gators and snakes. Bird flew around and would occasionally disappear but always returned to Sammy's side. Sammy thought about the many hours that slaves had spent digging and cleaning the canals and operating the trunks to flood the rice fields.

The sun was getting higher in the sky, and the day was going to be scorching. If anyone should come along, his simple plan was to hide in the brush or the fields. But he was so interested in keeping watch for snakes and gators that he was startled when he heard a voice.

"Boy, wha'choo doin' out here by yo'self? You ain't got no business here, and don't you tell me no lie. I be knowing if you lie to me."

Sammy had not been a runaway for a full day and already had been caught. "My pa is takin' produce to Geo'town," he said. "Massa is movin' cause he can't stand the heat, and he don't want no swamp fever."

"Where's yo' pa now?"

"I don't know. I had to do my business, and Pa pulled up onto the bank. I done it, but I lost my way back. When I finally found my way to the river, Pa was gone. I reckon he figgered I'd find my way back, or maybe he just didn't think one li'l black boy mattered. I know he's on his way to Geo'town. You goin' that way?"

"Yep, I got a load of cypress here. I'm polin' it down to Geo'town. Already got it sold, but I got to get it there. You think you can use a pole?" The man showed Sammy the way he put the pole in the water and walked to the back of the boat. That would propel the scow forward.

Sammy had seen boats either rowed or poled but had never done either.

"You can help me go to Geo'town, but I got to see yo' paper. You got a paper, don't ya?" When any slave left the plantation, he had to have a signed paper from his master. Without it, he was designated a runaway.

"Pa's got my papers, and he's on his way down the river."

The man looked skeptical. He scratched his beard and gave Sammy a hard look for several minutes. "Well, I could use the help, and iffen you can find yo' pa, I'll take you to town."

Sammy climbed aboard the scow as the man pushed it away from the bank. He was happy to feel dry wood beneath his feet instead of soggy mud. With the help of the current, the boat moved a considerable distance. They made slow but steady progress downriver. In the evening, they put into a small creek. Sammy gathered twigs and branches and other deadwood for the fire. He learned that the man's name was Enos. He had some fatback to fry and some corn to parch. Sammy shared the rest of his biscuits, and they slept on the boat. Sammy noticed Bird was roosting in a dense pine thicket. If Enos had noticed the colorful bird, he hadn't commented on its presence.

By noon the next day, they were passing the wharfs of Georgetown. Enos found the chandler's store that had ordered the cypress and tied up. Enos climbed a ladder up to the wharf from the low-riding scow. Sammy followed.

When Sammy reached the wharf, Enos instantly grabbed him by the back of the neck and twisted his ear so hard that he almost pulled it off.

He looked at the chandler and shouted, "I done got me a genuwine runaway here. You reckon the sheriff will pay me somethin' fo' this brat? He ain't much, but I'd stake my cypress haul that he's a runaway from upriver."

CHAPTER NINE

Sammy had been cautious and had not trusted Enos. He had planned to part ways with the thin man as soon as possible, but Enos had recognized the promise of an easy payday. He knew even a child runaway such as this Sammy could put some coin in his pocket.

The sheriff was summoned. He came by but didn't seem too interested. He was almost sympathetic to the scrawny child. He had undoubtedly run from a local plantation, but without outside support, he would not survive. "That there is some mean desperado you're holdin'. You sure you can handle him yourself, or do you want me to fetch a posse if you're scairt?"

Enos let the sheriff's sarcasm pass over him, or perhaps he didn't realize the insult he had just encountered. "Now look here, Sheriff. This here's a runaway slave, and I don't reckon that the size makes that less so. He's a might measly, but he's one hundred percent runaway slave, I guarantee!"

"Well, Mister…"

"Enos, my name is Enos."

"Well, Enos, we've got the patrollers who take care of runaways, and they'll be around and decide what to do with this one here. They'll find who he belongs to and see that he gets returned and decide on just what reward is due, Mister… Mister…"

"Enos, my name is Enos."

....

Further along the waterfront, where the water was deeper and the river was wider, oceangoing ships were moored. One of those ships was the *Mirabelle*. The *Mirabelle*'s master was Captain Domingo Mendoza.

Mendoza was taking a late-morning cup of tea on the foredeck of his handsome topsail schooner. The morning sun and gentle breeze off the ocean made him happy that he would be leaving on the next tide this very afternoon. He had profitably disposed of his cargo and restored his provisions in preparation for getting back out to sea. He was making big plans for his ventures with *Mirabelle*, but he still had some need of crewmen. He needed a crew with few family ties. He needed men who would not be missed if they disappeared at sea because his new venture would put both the ship and the crew in peril.

From the corner of his eye, Mendoza caught a glimpse of color on the portside gunwale amidships. There, perched on the port rail, was the scarlet macaw he had sold to the Hiatt plantation last spring. Hiatt had been so pleased to take possession of the bird. Mendoza should have warned Hiatt that he couldn't treat the bird as though it was one of his slaves. He could not imagine what the bird was doing back here without his master or other attendant. Things must not have gone well with the training process.

He put down his cup of tea and descended to the deck level, where the bird had alighted. "What are you doing here, amigo?"

The parrot sidestepped down the railing as the captain moved closer. Finally, Mendoza almost grasped the parrot, but it took a short flight to a stack of barrels on the wharf. The captain was intrigued. It seemed as though the parrot was asking to be followed. Since he had a few hours before the tide changed, he decided that he could use a last stroll on solid ground. As he approached the stack of barrels on the wharf, the bird flew further upriver. Once again, he perched clearly in sight, this time on the edge of the roof of a tavern.

44

After they repeated this process several times, Mendoza saw what he suspected was the reason for the bird's behavior. There was the little boy that Hiatt had called "the whistler," squatting on the wharf between the local constable, a poor human specimen from the backwoods, a third man that Mendoza recognized as the local chandler, and a burly man with long tangled hair, beard and a broad-brimmed hat. Mendoza suspected that the latter man was a member of the patrollers. He had encountered patrollers on occasion and usually found they were men unfit for most honest work.

He approached the group with an air of authority. "Well, young man, what brings you to Georgetown?" He spoke directly to the young black boy rather than the adults.

"I'm here to meet my pa. We got separated on the way over here."

Enos said to Mendoza, "This one's a runaway. He'll be worth some cash on the barrelhead when this here patroller figures it out."

Mendoza countered, "I know this young man. If his father is around, I don't see him as a runway at all. He's a lost little boy."

Enos responded, "Well, he ain't got no papers, and I don't see no lost pa, so that makes him a runaway."

Mendoza remembered Hiatt's name for the child. "This is Sambo, and his father suspected that on his first time in Georgetown, he might get lost, so we got Master Hiatt to write a paper for me to keep in case something like this happened."

The patroller said, "You produce the papers, and we'll release the boy to you till either his pa or Master Hiatt shows up."

Mendoza hurried back to the ship and went straight to his cabin. He opened the drawer in which he kept both the logbook and the account book. He found a slip of official-looking paper: the receipt for the parrot. It was clearly signed by Hiatt.

On this date, the year of our lord, April Twenty-first, eighteen hundred and twelve, one item being a viable animal is delivered.
J. T. Hiatt

Mendoza took a moment to examine the paper. Should he try to deceive the authorities for the sake of a slave boy he had seen for only a few hours months ago, or should he call this encounter a mistake, forget about getting involved, and leave on the outgoing tide? The child appeared to be frightened and if returned to the plantation would face severe punishment. The bird seemed devoted to the boy. That was the deciding factor.

Mendoza took the paper, placed it on the deck, stepped on it, and rolled it under his heel.

A minute later, he rejoined the men on the wharf and handed over the paper.

"What's this?" asked the patroller. Mendoza noticed tobacco stains down his unyielding beard. The stains extended from his beard down the front of his shirt to the waist.

"That's the permission for the boy to be off the plantation with his pa."

The patroller turned the paper first one-way and then another. Mendoza could see that the patroller was having difficulties reading the paper. Either the soiled paper was making the task difficult, or he was just unable to read. Mendoza thought the latter was more likely.

Finally, he handed the paper back to Mendoza. "All right, Captain, you can take the young'un with you-- and good riddance. Hiatt is a fool to coddle his slaves and let them run around. Discipline is what they need. Take this li'l runt. He ain't worth my trouble."

Mendoza helped the boy stand up. As he did, he tried to remember the child's real name. He would have to straighten that out later. "Now come with me, and we'll get some food into you and find your pa."

Mendoza led the boy along the wharf's narrow passage between all manner of freight and maritime hardware. When they were out of earshot of Enos, the sheriff, and the patroller, Sammy looked up at the captain. "I ain't got no pa to look for."

Mendoza kept walking and simply said, "I know."

CHAPTER TEN

Aboard the *Mirabelle*, Mendoza took Sammy to his cabin. He had the cook set a table, and the boy dined on biscuits, molasses, butter, eggs, and milk. The boy initially was too timid to eat, but he soon attacked his first decent meal in two days.

When the pace of the child's intake seemed to be slowing down, Captain Mendoza began to question the boy. "So, whistler boy, what do I call you? What exactly is your name?"

The boy looked up. Mendoza could tell he was thinking. Finally, he said, "Johnny. My name is Johnny."

Mendoza could have sworn that his name was probably Sambo or Sammy, but if he wanted to be Johnny, that was fine. "What are you doing away from the plantation?"

"I took a biscuit from the massa's basket. I was so hungry I couldn't help it."

"Did you quit whistling?"

"No, sir. Bird started helpin' me whistle."

Sammy, who now was taking the identity of his dead brother Johnny, knew he had to trust someone, and Captain Mendoza seemed like a good person—and the only person he could confide in. He told the captain the story of Massa's inability to train or kill the parrot and how he and the bird had developed a relationship that had led to the deception of the massa's family. He mentioned his brother's recent death but did not elaborate on the change in his identity.

"Well, Johnny, what do we do now? Would you like to stay with me?"

"You mean here, on the boat?"

"Ship. This is a ship. A boat is smaller. I need a cabin boy and will be going to sea on the outgoing tide. You want the job?"

"I be yo' slave?"

"I don't have slaves on the *Mirabelle*. My crew is paid. Now a cabin boy doesn't get much pay, but I'd wager it's more than you'd ever see with Master Hiatt."

"Can Bird come?"

Mendoza opened the cabin hatch and looked across the deck. Sure enough, the parrot was sitting on the bowsprit. "You call him Bird. Is that his name?"

The boy thought a moment. "I call him Bird. He's become my bird."

"You know, he is a macaw—that's a sort of parrot. He's your friend, so if it doesn't become confusing, calling him Bird is good. But he is free, just like you are now. If he stays with us, we'll find a place for him. If he doesn't follow or wants to leave, he will be free to do so."

Johnny thought about this. *Free.* He had heard this word before but never thought of it as anything but a word in a song. "Am I free?"

Mendoza almost said "free as a bird," but that didn't seem appropriate. Instead, he said, "You can be as free as you want to be. You'll be free of the plantation, free of Massa Hiatt, but beyond that, we'll see."

Johnny felt that was good enough. After all, he had no other choice. "That sounds fair enough, and yes, we'll see."

"Johnny, do you know what type of ship this is?"

"You take cargo and deliver it?"

"Yes, we pick up cargo, and we deliver it or sometimes sell it. We do other things as well."

"What kind of things?"

"Have you ever heard of privateers?"

CHAPTER ELEVEN

"Johnny, there's a war coming, and our side is at a disadvantage on the seas. American ships get pulled aside as they mind their own business, and the bully Brits take seamen off our ships and force them to serve on British ships. That's called impressment. Now do you think that's right?"

Sammy, now Johnny, was even more confused. "They make them their slaves? Is that wrong? Momma says our pappys was taken from far away and brought here without no say. Was that right?"

"No, Johnny, there is a lot in the world that isn't right. And we each can correct only a little at a time. I can help a little. I can hurt the Brits and help to right a little wrong. Will you help?" Mendoza knew the boy had nowhere to go, but he wanted the boy to commit again to the sea life.

"Uh, I guess. Can I bring Bird?"

"Bird will be welcome, but we need to get him below till we're out of sight."

"I think if we leave the door…"

"It is a door, but on a ship, we call it a hatch."

"If we keep the hatch open, and I whistle, Bird will come to me."

With the cabin opened to the deck, Johnny began to whistle "Old Dan Tucker." After a few bars, the parrot fluttered into the room and alighted on the corner of Mendoza's desk.

In a few minutes, one of the mates announced to the captain that the tide was now outgoing. Mendoza stood and turned to leave his cabin. "Now, Johnny, stay here with the parrot till we are out of sight of the land. Then come out on the deck, and we'll introduce you to the cook. You'll take orders from him. And you will sleep in the galley. I'll have plenty more for you to do, but that is a start. Now I've got new crewmen, and we've refitted *Mirabelle* to give her some teeth."

Mendoza began giving orders to cast off and push away from the wharf as other sailors prepared to hoist sails. The deck became a flurry of activity as sailors pulled on ropes—they called them sheets—and climbed in the rigging to release the sails.

Johnny felt the ship initially move sideways and then begin some forward momentum. He began to see the buildings moving by the portholes.

As the *Mirabelle* was just gaining the channel, Mendoza noticed a commotion along the wharf. The old man, the patroller, and the sheriff were running down the wharf, waving at the ship. Behind them was the plantation owner, Hiatt.

He heard Hiatt yell, "You've got my property! You've got Sambo in there, and you've got my parrot! Now heave to and tie up, then we'll let you leave."

The *Mirabelle* was gaining speed as the channel deepened and the wind began to fill the sails. Mendoza saw the commotion on the wharf, but felt he was beyond their reach. He shrugged his shoulders and gestured that he couldn't understand them.

Hiatt cupped his hands and yelled even louder. "Sambo! You've got my slave boy, Sambo!"

Mendoza waited a moment to consider this and yelled back, "Johnny, my new cabin boy is Johnny!"

Hiatt yelled again through cupped hands, "Where's my bird?"

Mendoza was now almost beyond hailing distance but gave one last shout. "The shore is full of birds. Pick one!"

Hiatt was already winded by the uncustomary exertion, and his florid face became even redder with fury at the impudence of the captain. He kicked a barrel so hard that he lost his balance and fell flat on his back. The obese master flopped down like a turtle stranded on its back.

Shortly, *Mirabelle* crossed the breakwater and was in open water. Mendoza used his spyglass to examine the wharf area and did not see any evidence of boats being launched. He gave orders for his crew to trim the sails and set a course for Bermuda.

....

Johnny became the cook's helper, doing many of the same jobs that he had done for Momma and Massa. He was now experiencing a life he had never imagined on the plantation. Once he had overcome his initial seasickness, the salt air and the ocean had become his friends. He had watched the shorebirds till the *Mirabelle* was well offshore. Then he had begun watching the water. He saw a pod of fish swim beside the ship. Cook said they were not fish but porpoises. There was a myth that sometimes they were part woman and part fish, but Cook had never seen one like that.

The water changed into a deep blue color that Cook explained was the Gulf Stream. Cook and the captain began to explain the tides and currents to him, but after being on the plantation for all his life, Johnny found all of this new and had difficulty comprehending the complexity of the sea. It would be a continuing process.

He watched the sailors go about their duties and puzzled at the practice of handling the cannons. He remembered Massa Hiatt remarking to Captain Mendoza that the captain had increased his armament, but wondered if he needed four cannons for defense. Several of the sailors practiced loading and firing the guns. Several other sailors used pistols and long guns. They also practiced using long knives that they called swords. This was in addition to the routine attention to the helm and the sails, which continually needed to be trimmed.

A week into the voyage, a seaman atop the main sail shouted, "Sail ho!"

A course was set to intercept the vessel the seaman had spotted. But the captain was concerned about the weather. He watched the hand of a gauge in an instrument on the wall. "There's a blow coming. We may lose the prize."

Johnny noticed that the sea was no longer gently rolling but kicking up whitecaps, with waves of such large size that they began to break over the deck. The lookout, one of Mendoza's new crewmen, nearly fell and came down from his perch in the rigging.

Mendoza ordered, "Get back up on your watch. We'll lose the prize if we can't close on it. This weather will help, as he likely reefed his sails to ride out the storm."

"I can't balance on the rigging. I'll surely fall to my death if you make me go back."

Johnny was reminded of his tall pine tree hideout on the plantation. "I'll go. I'll find them sails fo' you."

"Son, you're too little to look out. You can't go up there alone," the captain responded.

"I won't be alone. I'll take Bird."

Johnny's parrot had become the ship's pet. He mostly perched in either the captain's cabin or the galley with Johnny. He would take flight and circle the lower main sail before alighting on the gunwale, but he never ventured high or far. Now Johnny wanted to take the highest lookout post with the assistance of the parrot.

Before Mendoza could complain further, Johnny began to climb up the rigging. The rope was now wet and slippery. The rocking of the boat reminded Johnny of a cork float on his fishing line when a big carp was hungry for a worm. As the squall passed over the ship, the rain began to burn Johnny's skin and eyes, but he continued to climb. Bird flew ever-tightening circles about the boy.

He reached the level of the schooner's main sail, but he couldn't see much more than he could from the deck. He ventured ever higher, and soon, he was at the level of the topsail spar. Once he got to the topsail spar, he held tight to the mast and straddled the spar.

The captain watched the climb with a sense of horror. He had become fond of the boy, and though he likely could better afford to lose the waif than one of his more able-bodied seamen, he didn't want him hurt.

In spite of the wind and rain stinging his eyes, Johnny gazed at the horizon as much as he could. Finally, there was a break in the rain, and he thought he saw a dot on the horizon just off the port bow. He shouted as though he were an experienced lookout. "Sail ho, off the port bow!"

The captain clapped his hands and turned the ship to the port side. "Well done! Can you stay there longer?"

Johnny was hanging on for his life and did not feel he could safely come down even if he wanted to, but he responded as he felt a real sailor would. "Aye, Captain!"

Mendoza yelled again, "Good boy. Now let us know if she changes course."

Johnny was unsure whether his fear was abated by his pride at having pleased Mendoza or by the fact that the storm was passing, but he was able to slightly loosen his grip on the mast. Bird still had his claws burrowed securely in the topsail spar and was not likely to be dislodged.

Soon he was able to report. "Sail still to port, but larger."

The captain asked, "Is he at full sail? And how many masts?"

Johnny continued using his newly found nautical speech. "His top sails are furled, and his main sail is reefed. I see two masts."

The captain felt that a two-master ship would likely be a merchant packet ship. She would not likely be heavily armed. This could be the type of trophy he was looking for.

CHAPTER TWELVE

Johnny kept a watch on the ship and regularly reported the position. The storm gradually subsided, though the sea remained rough. The *Mirabelle* was under full sail as it pursued the targeted ship. The sailors were all on deck. It was less uncomfortable there than below deck in spite of the spray.

Finally, there was increased commotion on the deck as the captain announced that he could easily see the ship in the spyglass. He shouted up into the rigging, "Johnny, good job. You can come down now."

Johnny tried to release his grip on the mast but found that his hands were cramped onto it, and it took some time to get them loose. His legs were trembling so much that he had problems finding the loops of rope that made the rigging.

As he was coming down from the perch, a seaman passed him on the way to the mainsail spar. He had a long gun strapped to his back. As he passed Johnny, he too acknowledged the young man's work. "Good job, mate!"

Now that Johnny was a "mate," his cramps seemed to ease, and his spirits soared.

Finally, the ship was in hailing distance. The captain raised a megaphone and shouted, "Ahoy there! Heave to for boarding."

The ship did not change its sails, alter course, or return the captain's hailing. Instead the ship ran up the Union Jack standard, indicating it was a British ship, protected by the greatest navy in the world.

In response to this, Captain Mendoza raised the pennant of an American registration. He had the crew charge the deck cannons and prepare to fire. At the same time, he brought the *Mirabelle* about until it was parallel to the British ship.

The British captain decided that now was a good time to hail the upstart American ship that had been harassing him. "Ahoy, American vessel. This is British vessel *Odette*. We are under protection of the British Empire. You will let us pass unimpeded."

Captain Mendoza had planned for this response. "*Odette*, again, heave to for boarding to search for American seamen, or we will fire on you."

There was no change in the course or pace of the British vessel.

Now Johnny could see that the entire crew of the vessel was on deck—and making violent and obscene gestures toward the *Mirabelle.* Some even sat on the ship's rail and lowered their pants, exposing their backsides to the American vessel. Johnny had never experienced anything even close to this. He was scared but also more excited than he'd thought he could be, and he had played at least a small part in making this happen. Bird was also excited. He flew a circle over the *Mirabelle*, alighted close to Johnny's side, shifted his weight from one leg to another, fluffed up his plumage about his neck and chest, and then repeated the flight. He did this over and over.

The captain allowed the arrogant behavior of the *Odette*'s crew to proceed long enough for the Brits to evaluate their situation. Soon they changed course to veer away from the *Mirabelle*. The American ship matched the course of the target and soon was again in cannon range.

Captain Mendoza commanded, "Put a shot across her bow."

The bow gun crew made adjustments in the cannon's position and barrel angle. They placed chocks beneath the wheels and lit the fuse. The captain placed his hands over his ears, and Johnny did the same.

Bam! The cannon's roar was easily the loudest noise Johnny had ever heard, even with his hands over his ears. There was a splash one ship's length in front of the British ship's bow.

The *Odette* made no immediate response, but it was soon evident that as a merchant ship, she didn't have the armaments to match the *Mirabelle*. This time, the British captain's voice seemed to communicate more resignation than arrogance. He denied that there were any impressed American sailors on the ship, but he would heave to for inspection. He considered it an act of piracy.

The two ships were lashed together, and a boarding party including Captain Mendoza boarded the *Odette*. Johnny was ordered to stay with the cook, who doubled as a medical person in the case of injuries. Bird took to flight and circled above both of the ships, swooping through the rigging of the ships.

The first step was to disarm the ship. All firearms were collected, along with swords, knives, daggers, and anything else that could be reasonably used as a weapon. All of the crew was questioned regarding nationality and whether they were there under duress. There were two Americans who reported that they had been involuntarily removed from an American packet ship and impressed into duty on a British frigate—a mighty armed warship—but they had since been transferred to this smaller vessel. They had been looking for an opportunity to jump ship but were relieved for the rescue. Then, like the crew of a true privateer, the men of the *Mirabelle* searched the vessel for valuables. They held the captain at dagger point as the safe was emptied. The galley was relieved of fresh vegetables and casks of water. The cargo hold was examined, and the tobacco was removed, along with rice, silver furnishings, glass panes, and tea.

After two hours, the *Mirabelle* crew was ready to take its leave. Captain Mendoza calculated that the British ship had just enough provisions to reach Bermuda if they had good weather for two or three days.

The two ships were unlashed, and the *Mirabelle* veered away from the British ship and sailed in the direction opposite Bermuda.

Johnny had spent the entire time with the cook in the galley, awaiting injuries to treat. He asked, "What happens now?"

The cook was relieved. "Now we put the supplies away, be sure that everything is in good order for the next time, and swab the deck."

"Does anyone ever get hurt?"

"Johnny, what color is this floor?"

Johnny naively answered, "It's a red floor."

"Yes, Johnny, 'cause we never get the color of blood out, no matter how hard we try. I pray to the saints that you never see how bad it can be."

Still curious, Johnny asked, "What happens to what we took from them?"

"We'll put the American sailors ashore if we ever get back to shore. They'll be part of the crew till then, and who knows—the captain may offer them a berth. The captain will sort through the booty and put it in the ship stores or sell it at our next port. We all get a share, some more than others. Even a brave cabin boy will get a share. Surely, it's a small share, but—"

"Do you mean that I may get paid?"

"Why, Johnny, you stick wit' the captain long 'nough, and you may be able to buy that plantation you came from. Yeah, we know you were a plantation boy, but Captain Mendoza has a good sense about people. His approval is alls I need."

CHAPTER THIRTEEN

The *Mirabelle* was now loaded. The hold was full, and barely any powder had been depleted from the magazine. Captain Mendoza also had two new seamen. The seamen, by their account, had been illegally taken from American ships to fill the roster of the British navy. They were so grateful that they were eager to join Mendoza's crew. The captain would have preferred to rove the Gulf Stream longer, but the *Mirabelle* was slow and less agile with the extra tonnage. Plus, he had commitments that needed to be fulfilled on the mainland.

Mendoza set a course for Charleston. On the return voyage, Johnny assumed the role of cabin boy, plus part-time lookout. He eagerly embraced this duty since it was something the able-bodied seamen did. Bird flew about the mast and would alight on the spar or rigging as Johnny scanned the horizon for sails. On the return, Mendoza was hoping not to see any. He wanted to dispose of his booty before some other privateer could make him a victim.

Charleston Harbor was much larger than Georgetown. It was bustling with ships and filled with dandies as well as common folks. There was no lack of slaves. After the crew had tied up to a pier for disembarking, the cook remarked on a commotion in the square just past the waterfront. Johnny was anxious to disembark from the *Mirabelle*, but the cook told—or perhaps ordered—him to stay on board. He heard bidding and got glimpses of the activity through breaks in the crowd. He saw a black man standing on a platform. His skin had been oiled and shined up till it glistened, and he was naked. Men were looking at him as though he was a prize calf or mule. After the bidding finished, the auctioneer pounded a hammer on his desk and yelled, "Sold!" The man was removed from the stage and placed in shackles, and the process repeated again for the next person. Johnny had seen enough.

He went below to the galley and sat at the table. Cook gave him a plate with boiled peanuts and sat down with him. "I'm sorry you saw a slave auction. Selling men doesn't seem right, does it?"

"Massa Hiatt never sold nobody. I never heard of him buyin' no one neither, but when I was in the house, I heard them bank people talk about him borrowing so much he might have to sell them black folks. I reckon that was us."

Mendoza returned to the ship with three men. They were real dandies, with tall hats and fancy coats whose coattails extended down the backs of their britches to their knees.

Cook said one was Governor Alston, and the others were agents. "The governor gave the captain a 'letter of marque and reprisal," said the cook. "That more or less makes us legal to retrieve our sailors and get a bit of booty from the Brits and their friends. We call that the spoils of war. That's so we don't get hung as pirates. We get to sell our booty legally, and the governor there gets a cut. Some privateers will burn the ships and send the survivors off in a boat if they're lucky. I've never seen Captain do that. If he gets enough crew, he may take a ship as a prize and sell it in port, but he ain't done that yet neither."

"Do you think he'd sell me?"

"Nah, boy, he ain't gonna sell you, and he ain't gonna sell or cook that bird neither. Why, you're a regular sailor now, and he had eyes on that bird ever since it came aboard in Cozumel. You got a home here, boy."

Johnny thought about this. He knew this statement would be with him for a long time. He regretted that he could not tell his momma that he was doing well in his new home.

The crew enjoyed themselves in town that night and returned to the ship as the sun was rising over the offshore islands. They appeared to be impaired by rum, lack of sleep, or both.

Captain was in no mood to let them rest. He immediately ordered them to begin getting the ship ready to return to the sea. "There's profit to be made," the captain said, "and the Brits are ripe for the picking. Our letter is dated before the *Odette*, so we're all legal. Let's get back to sea!"

CHAPTER FOURTEEN

The *Mirabelle* had fair winds and a following sea upon departing Charleston. The ship's earlier quick success near Bermuda waters encouraged Captain Mendoza to return to those waters.

Johnny and Bird were beginning to adjust to the routines of a cabin boy's demanding life. Johnny's main duties were to help the cook, to see that Captain Mendoza's meals were on time if he ate in his cabin, and to make sure his boots were clean and his clothes straight.

Johnny now had the added duties of lookout, which he enjoyed. When he had climbed the tall pines around the slave quarters, he could stay nestled in the upper branches of the trees for hours. His momma would call for him repeatedly and be at her wits' end until she remembered to look high up, at which point she would see him in a tall pine waving in the wind. While in the tree, he would look toward the ocean and enjoy the sway of the pine in even mild breezes. The lookout duties reminded him of those times. He would find a comfortable position on the spar of the topsail, and Bird would perch near him. He talked to Bird as he would have talked to his brother. Bird was a good listener. He gyrated his head as though he were conversing with a friend.

Johnny whistled just as he had on the plantation, not only to fight off boredom but also to hear Bird join in the serenade. The crew began to look forward to the whistling lookout and his feathered partner.

Five days into the voyage, Johnny saw a sail on the horizon. He yelled, "Sail ho," just as he had been instructed, and he was grateful that he had fought off the boredom enough to see the tiny sail so far away.

The captain ordered a course change, and the chase of predator and prey began. After hours of tacks and jibs, the *Mirabelle* was close enough to hail the ship.

The captain used his megaphone to announce his intentions. "Ahoy there. This is Captain Mendoza of the United States Ship *Mirabelle*. Heave to, and prepare to be boarded."

The captain of the opposing ship responded, "This is Captain Ames of His Majesty's Ship *Sylvie*. I have no intention of allowing boarding by you or any American."

Mendoza called an order to the first gunner. "Put a five-pounder across her bow."

"Aye, Captain."

The cannon fired, and once again Johnny covered his ears to reduce the ear ringing and pain associated with the explosion. The round once again hit a few yards in front of the bow. Rather than heaving to, the *Sylvie* loosed her own barrage. Two cannons were fired almost at the same time. Johnny saw one coming directly at him. He had no time to move or even react to the cannonball. He felt the heat of the hot cannonball swish by his cheek as it ripped a hole in the topsail and landed in the water on the far side of the *Mirabelle*, splashing water and steam high in the air and dousing the far side of the ship.

The *Sylvie*'s second cannon fire was more effective. It smashed through the near gunwale and proceeded across the deck of the *Mirabelle*, cutting down two sailors and destroying structures and rigging before plowing through the deck and gunwale on the opposite side. The first sailor in the path of destruction lay still in a puddle of his own blood. His left arm was separated from his body and hung loose in his sleeve. The left side of his chest was caved in. There was no movement from the dead body.

This was the first death Johnny had encountered since his brother's. His brother had appeared peaceful and almost like he was sleeping, with no distortion of his features, but the sailor's body was terribly deformed. Johnny knew that he likely should look away, but he couldn't until his attention was diverted to the second injured man. The cannonball had ripped his left leg from his body about six inches below the knee. He was howling and jerking the shortened leg as it spurted a river of blood across the deck. Cook rushed to his side immediately and began pulling the man back into the galley by his shoulders. As he moved along the deck, he looked up at Johnny and yelled, "Get down here! We need you!"

The noise on the ship was so loud that Johnny couldn't hear the cook's words, but his intent was obvious. Johnny scrambled down the damaged rigging as quickly as possible. Bird circled him as he made his way down and into the galley. When he entered, the cook already had the injured sailor on a table, with a rope tightly wrapped around the leg above the stump. The cook had wedged a marlinspike beneath the rope.

"Here, hold this tight, and twist it till the blood stops," the cook said as he turned away.

Johnny twisted the spike as tightly as possible. The sailor initially protested, but his protests rapidly turned feeble. His color was pallid, reminding Johnny of his brother's color in death.

When the cook turned around again, he had a red-hot poker in his hand. He immediately pressed the end of the poker on and into the wound. As he did, he commented, "It's a good thing he's passed out. This is too much to take otherwise." The beefy stump sizzled as steam and smoke arose from the wound. The odor of seared flesh permeated the room, but the bleeding had slowed to a mild trickle. "Keep that tourniquet tight even if he comes to and tries to take it off," said the cook. "We'll loosen it after a while."

Johnny suspected that the man would be dead long before any loosening was required.

Cook looked to Johnny and said, "It looks like the fat cow Captain was chasing turned out to be a raging bull. You stay put here. I'll be back with more work in a minute." The noise was already deafening, and as Cook opened the hatch to exit the galley, a massive boom shook the whole ship.

Captain had ordered two cannons into action. One shot was aimed at the quarterdeck, where the captain would likely be. That shot destroyed the deck and mortally injured *Sylvie*'s Captain Ames. The second shot hit one of her cannons. The weapon and crew disappeared into the new hole in the deck. In a moment, further explosions shook the *Sylvie* and sent a surge of heat over the water to the *Mirabelle*. The cook guessed that the damage of the second shot had ignited some powder on the deck beneath the cannon.

The ships were close enough that grappling hooks could be thrown across, and boarding began. The *Sylvie*'s crew was now eager to drop their weapons and submit to the boarders.

Captain Mendoza walked across the deck and knelt beside the dying Captain Ames. "You put up a courageous fight, Captain."

Captain Ames was barely able to speak. "We had a good run… had a lot to fight for."

"You fought for your life."

"Spanish gold is a big incentive."

"You're carrying Spanish gold?"

There was no answer from Ames. He was gone.

Mirabelle's crew began transferring treasure, cargo, and stores. They also were busy tending to the injured and fighting to keep the disabled *Sylvie* afloat.

Johnny and the cook were busy with injured crewmen of both ships. The boy now amply understood why the floor was painted red. It was currently covered in a syrupy substance with the acrid metallic odor of blood and powder.

In spite of the frantic activity in the galley, a sailor handed a message to the cook. Cook turned to Johnny. "The captain wants you back up top. He wants some sharp eyes on the horizon. We're making a lot of flames and smoke. And sound carries for miles on the open sea. We may be attracting attention."

Johnny was happy to leave the galley for the relative peace of the topsail. The lookout post that he had made into a sort of nest for himself was relatively unscathed. There was a big tear in the sail with scorched borders that would need to be repaired later, and the spar didn't seem as stable as before, but he felt secure enough. Smoke was obscuring much of his view and burned his eyes. His constant companion, Bird, had his claws firmly implanted in the spar beside Johnny.

Captain Mendoza was busy searching the dead captain's cabin. His desk contained the *Sylvie*'s letter of marque from the governor of Bermuda. Captain Mendoza realized he had pursued another privateer, a treasure hunter such as himself. The *Sylvie* had been commissioned not as a weapon against the British, like Mendoza, but to impoverish the Spanish, who had long been a thorn in the side of the British Empire.

The captain's log revealed that the *Sylvie* had encountered a Spanish treasure ship following a hurricane. The Spanish ship had taken the worst of the storm and was damaged. She was barely able to make headway and was in need of significant repair. Captain Ames and the crew of the *Sylvie* had relieved the Spanish of their valuable treasure, before scuttling the ship and sending the crew off on boats. The *Sylvie* had experienced other encounters, but the treasure ship had been far and away the biggest prize. In the captain's cabin there were two large trunks and a smaller armored box. Using keys taken from the dead captain, Mendoza first opened the large trunks and found a fortune in gold and silver coins. The smaller sealed box was filled with jewels. There were emerald-encrusted crosses, tiaras, necklaces, bracelets, and other jewelry. There were bags of loose precious stones not set in jewelry. These were all nested among gold coins.

Mendoza had just finished storing the booty from the captain's cabin in his own quarters aboard the *Mirabelle* when he heard the voice of his lookout, Johnny. "Sail ho on the port side!"

A sail appeared on the horizon. Ordinarily, this would be a welcome event for any privateer, but Mendoza was afraid that he had kicked a hornet's nest by taking a ship with a Bermuda letter of marque, which was equivalent to attacking the British Empire.

No sooner had Mendoza considered this than he heard Johnny yet again. "Two sails ho off the port!"

The captain looked up at Johnny high up in the rigging and questioned, "Can you see the number of masts?"

Johnny answered, "I can't tell for sure, but it looks like two masts per ship. There may be more."

Mendoza had no stomach for more combat in the next day. He commanded his crew to set a course for Charleston as hastily as possible. As the ship was pushed away from the *Sylvie*, the sails were set and trimmed, and the *Mirabelle* began tacking into the wind for Charleston.

As the *Mirabelle* began to make progress in her departure, Mendoza looked back at the ill-fated *Sylvie*. She was settling heavily into the water. He hoped that the vessels Johnny had spotted would arrive in time to help the sinking ship. He wished from a humanitarian standpoint that the ship would be saved. He also hoped that the time needed to assist the *Sylvie* would give the *Mirabelle* time to escape.

Mendoza weighed the odds to help him make a decision. Action on the open sea against a British warship of the line would not be good for the *Mirabelle*. He needed to avoid that confrontation.

Mendoza was gazing out at the sea in the direction that the sails had been spotted. On the wall of the cabin was a barometer. The needle was dropping by the hour.

CHAPTER FIFTEEN

Mendoza was not able to see the sails, but Johnny saw them from the top of the mast. He had to assume that the British lookout would be gazing in his direction.

On deck the crew was trimming the sails to put on as much speed as possible, tacking and jibing a staggered course to the west. The sails and rigging were repaired even as the ship was running on the edge of the wind to gain every bit of speed possible. The vessel was tilted at an uncomfortable level for the crew, and Johnny's perch was tilted at such an angle that he was looking down over water rather than to the deck below. Now Johnny could see only one sail.

Mendoza realized that one ship was giving assistance to the crippled *Sylvie* while the second vessel was on the hunt for the predator. The sail had been no more than a speck on the horizon, but it seemed to be very slowly gaining in size. As the *Mirabelle* jigged and jagged to get the most efficient use of the wind, the view of sail moved from port to starboard and back.

The waves grew larger and now had deeper troughs and prevalent white caps. The sky became covered with dense clouds, and rain intermittently pelted the sails on a wind that came from the southeast. Johnny's perch was becoming slippery and uncomfortable in the rain.

The captain looked up at the boy and yelled, "Johnny, get down here. You've done well."

Mendoza knew Johnny was merely a child, but he had provided a valuable service, and now using his spyglass, he could see the sail himself. Under ordinary circumstances, Mendoza would have been reefing the sails and having the ship trimmed for running against severe weather, but with the risk of a British ship that was hell bent on revenge following them, *Mirabelle* needed all speed she could muster. Mendoza was inclined to trust that his ship was still seaworthy enough to withstand the stresses of a forced sail.

Waves were now breaking over the deck, and the splintered area was allowing water below deck. This put the ship in peril. Some of the crew attempted to repair the damaged deck with pitch, canvas, and anything else that might fill the gap.

Johnny was shivering below deck. Bird remained at his side. Cook had cleared the wounded from the galley. Even the sailor with the amputated leg had been moved below and was still among the living. The crew had made some effort to swab the floor, but the cook was unable to fix any sort of warm meal. The seas were just too rough. Cook gave Johnny a cup of something called *grog* and a thick slice of bread. He said, "You're a real seadog now."

Johnny drank the liquid, and it made him feel all-warm inside and even burned his throat and stomach a little, but he liked it. He poured out a bit for Bird and fed him pieces of the bread.

On deck, the captain was watching the storm and the approaching ship. The sails had now enlarged and were indeed on three masts. The hull also could be seen when the *Mirabelle* crested a wave, revealing that the ship was studded with two decks of gun ports. They were being followed by a ship of the line. It didn't appear to be as large as some British frigates, but it was still a formidable enemy. Their only chance was to outrun the warship. If the storm didn't get too bad and if the winds became more favorable, and if all the other factors fell into place, the *Mirabelle* might survive. There were so many ifs.

As yet, the ship was far out of gun range and was tacking on a course opposing the *Mirabelle*, so the wind could be the arbiter of who would win this battle.

The storm worsened in intensity. The wind was constantly shifting, and gusts were stressing the sails beyond their limits. In the dark, the dense cloud cover made for a starless night. The only light came from lightning flashes that seemed to be all around. The occasional flash from the east outlined the British man-of-war, which seemed ominously close.

As dawn approached, Mendoza's spyglass gave him a better view of the ship. He could see the sails clearly, he could make out figures of the crew on the deck, and even worse, he could see that the bow gun port was now open!

He saw a puff of whitish smoke from the forward gun port just before the ship disappeared in the trough of a wave. In seconds the boom of the cannon was heard above the blow of the wind and thunder. Then the cannonball whizzed past the bow and splashed harmlessly.

Mendoza altered course to reduce the profile of the ship, but this made the *Mirabelle* unstable in the face of a strong gale. Mendoza hoped that the opponent was having more difficulties getting positioned for its next shot. He knew that the captain must be extremely reckless or insane to open the gun ports for attempted shots in these seas.

When the lightning again flashed, the opposing ship was at the top of a wave, and a flash was seen from the second gun port. The sound was drowned out by a tremendous thunderclap. This time two cannonballs tethered by a chain flew through the rigging. The main mast was severed above the mainsail. Johnny's previous perch dropped over the side and began dragging off the starboard side of the ship. It was causing such a list in the ship that the waves were breaking over the rail.

A brave sailor started toward the rail to cut the rigging and drop the mast over the side. He slid down the deck to the tangle of rigging on the side of the ship. Several hacks later, he had the lines and tangled sheets separated and was ready to push the mass of debris over the railing. As he made the last great push to free the ship from the debris, the ship listed in a wave that completely covered the mid-deck, and the sailor and the debris were washed over the rail.

With the debris gone, the ship righted and rose on the next wave. The debris and the sailor were nowhere to be seen.

Cook was holding onto any fixed surface he could reach and having problems keeping his balance. By now, the ship was wallowing into troughs between waves so deep that the crests of the waves could not be seen above the hull. The ship could be directed by the foresail and rudder but was largely at the mercy of the wind.

Mendoza again looked in the direction of the British ship. The frequent flashes of lightning illuminated the surface but did not reveal the vessel.

CHAPTER SIXTEEN

Aboard the HMS *Margery*, First Mate Robert Dalton was concerned about the safety of his ship and the sanity of the captain. The *Margery* had been patrolling western Bermuda when smoke was sighted on the western horizon. The course had been changed to a western heading to the area of the smoke. A second British ship had come to assist in the investigation of the smoke.

Within hours, they had intercepted the *Sylvie* and discovered the ship was close to foundering. The *Sylvie* was boarded and deemed to be in immediate danger of sinking. The crew was removed, and one of the British ships stayed by the ill-fated *Sylvie* in a desperate attempt to reverse the below-decks flooding until the seas decided her fate. Then it would set a course for Bermuda. The *Margery* had left the scene to search for the ship identified as an American privateer called *Mirabelle.*

The weather had become menacing, but Captain Adams was a newly minted officer recently assigned to the command of the *Margery*, and like too many of the commanders in the British navy, he had been given a ship due to his family status and political contacts rather than his merit. Captain Adams was eager to show the might of the British navy in the North Atlantic.

Soon his alert lookouts were able to see faint smoke and a sail to the west. Weather was becoming a problem, but the *Margery* was a fine ship, with a strong history of managing severe weather. The ship set course to intercept the American privateer. To get the benefit of the wind and gain the most speed, a course of tacking was undertaken. Although the ship moved well, the rough seas and the gusting wind meant that the *Margery* was very uncomfortable. The galley was unable to prepare meals for the sailors, who were busy managing the sail trim on a complex system of a three-masted ship. Below deck, the gun crews were readying the cannons for imminent combat. The British ship of the line was gaining on the *Mirabelle*, which seemed to be experiencing worse weather and to have less ability to handle the wind.

First Mate Dalton informed Captain Adams that they were approaching the range of the *Margery*'s cannons but that the seas were too rough to open the gun ports or get accurate firing solutions. But Adams felt that the time for the cannon was now, and he ordered a cannon shot for range. The first shot had range, but the rough seas made the cannons barely manageable to load, and the ship was so unstable that accuracy suffered.

Then Captain Adams ordered a second cannon shot with tethered cannonballs—two cannonballs tethered together by a heavy chain. The shot was made to destroy rigging and personnel. Dalton protested, "Captain, the ship is not stable, and the gun ports aren't safe to be open. The whole ship could founder."

Adams was adamant. "Dalton, I want that cannon fire. I want to show that American what the British navy can do!"

Reluctantly, Dalton responded, "Aye, sir." It sickened him to give the order to reload the cannon and open the gun port amidships, but it was an order.

Below deck, the gun crews were wrestling the heavy cannons. The main cannoneer, John Bullware, was—as his name implied —a bull of a man. He had been overseeing gun crews for years. He knew well the dangers and challenges of handling heavy cannons and explosive powder in confined spaces. When the gale-force winds were factored in, Bullware became even more anxious. His crew lacked his experience. His second was a thin impressed American, Jones, taken from a packet ship and forced into duty by the British navy. His dedication to his duties on the gun deck was lukewarm at best. With new loading orders, the chocks had to be removed from the wheels of the cannon, which had to be winched back in the gun deck to give the crew room to reload the hot barrel after a cannon fire. The barrel had to be swabbed with a brush to remove any residue and then mopped with a special mop from a bucket of water hanging at each cannon, to kill any sparks and prevent an explosion as powder was placed in the barrel. With the cannon charged, a fuse was placed. The tethered cannonballs were placed in the barrel. Then the crew was ready to re-chock the wheels, open the gun port, and light the fuse. Additional buckets of water hung by the cannon due to the constant danger of fires.

The leader of the gun crew announced, "Ready to fire!" Dalton heard this and yelled it to Captain Adams in the roaring wind and horizontal rain.

Adams yelled, "Fire at will!"

Dalton could not hear the command, but he did see the captain's mouth move as he nodded his head in the affirmative. Dalton relayed this command to the gun crew.

When they felt the ship rise on a wave and pitch slightly to elevate the cannon muzzle, the crew opened the gun port. Tasks that usually took seconds to perform were slower in the face of an extreme blow. This was no exception. By the time the gun port was opened, the ship was rising up the crest of a wave and soon would begin to slide down into the trough.

Often the difference between success and tragedy could be measured in seconds or by a quirk of fate. Captain Adams's order could have been a stroke of genius that would have conquered the privateer, were it not for two factors. First, one of the gun crew had not adequately secured one wheel of the cannon. Second, a surprise wave generated by the storm hit the *Margery* broadside to starboard.

After the crew received the order to fire, they had to wait until the ship rose on a wave to give themselves time to open the port, fire the cannon, re-secure the cannon, and close the gun port before the ship again dipped into the sea. Finally, the ship began to rise, and the port was opened and the fuse lit. As the cannon fired, the leader of the gun crew, Bullware, realized that one wheel of the cannon was not completely chocked. He looked at Jones and cursed, but the damage was done.

The result was that after the cannon fired, rather than the expected recoil, it jerked to one side, wedging the muzzle into the open gun port. This crushed Jones and another crewman between the cannon carriage and the hull. With the cannon barrel tightly wedged in the gun port, the crew was unable to close the port against the incoming seas. They attempted vainly to pry the cannon loose while the gun deck began to flood. At that moment an enormous wave hit the ship on the starboard and rolled it to port, keeping the port side well below water level.

The captain and his first mate heard reports from the gun deck in horror. To make matters worse, if that was possible, the severe weather that had seemed to be worse for the *Mirabelle* was now moving to engulf the *Margery*.

When things went wrong aboard ships in strong gale-force winds, they went wrong quickly. This storm was no different. In minutes, the wallowing *Margery* suffered a series of immense waves breaking over its side, and the next monumental wave sent her to the bottom.

Had Captain Adams been more cautious, had the gun crew been more attentive, had seaman Jones not been an impressed American seaman, or had a thunderstorm not generated a series of gigantic waves to the starboard of the *Margery*, the outcome might have been different.

Captain Adams's arrogant strategy had failed because of one small oversight by the gun crew, a change in the weather, and the ego of a green, untrained commander. The admiralty would remark that the loss of the *Margery* was the result of a seasonal hurricane.

CHAPTER SEVENTEEN

Aboard the *Mirabelle*, Captain Mendoza was still hoping to weather the storm. The ship was being pushed to the west with very little steerage. All he could do was try to keep the bow into the waves to help stabilize the ship, but even if he had adequate helm control, the waves were in such a maelstrom that they were almost impossible to read. Mendoza had lost track of the British ship and could only imagine that its crew also had their hands full managing the storm. The barometer in his cabin now was at the lowest point he had seen. He realized that this was not just a strong gale but a full-fledged hurricane.

Johnny stayed with the cook. They tried to keep the galley from falling into complete disarray. The ship was riding lower in the water, and the captain gave the order to lighten it. Deck guns went over the side along with ship stores, cargo brought over from the *Sylvie*, and anything nonessential. Mendoza looked at the heavy chests in his cabin and began to consider his options.

The seas relentlessly pounded the *Mirabelle*. In spite of efforts to guide her in the general direction of Charleston, she was being driven to the northwest along the course of the hurricane. As dawn approached, the crew began to see debris passing along on the waves. Palm leaves, trees, and even some possible remnants of a ship were riding the crests of waves.

To the west a different sound was heard. The sound of surf pounding on a beach was unmistakable. The crew watched for a shoreline, but the dense rain impaired vision. Suddenly, with a brief break in the maelstrom, the green outline of an island or shore was noted.

The crew was optimistic, but soon they realized that the ship would be grounded and crushed in the surf. That had been the fate of many ships along this part of the coast.

As the ship was pushed broadside by the continual waves, there was an inevitable scraping sound as the keel first brushed a sandbar and finally jammed firmly against the obstacle. Sounds of stressed timbers and failing hatches were heard across the ship. The ship was now a fixed object that intensified the force of the wind's damage.

Mendoza made a decision. He took a quick inventory of his remaining crew and called the cook and his strongest boatman to his cabin. After some thought, he also called Johnny. He had developed a bond with the child and wanted to keep him safe, but he didn't know how.

"Take the chests," he said, pointing to the two big chests and the smaller chest in the corner of his cabin. "Put them in the long boat, lash them in, and go to shore. Hide them and keep them safe. They'll lighten us, and if we do lose the ship, we'll need them."

He didn't need to tell the seasoned sailors that if by some miracle they survived the storm and the others on the ship did not, they would have the treasure, but they knew that was what he meant.

"Time is short," he said. "Let's get to it."

When they again went on deck, they saw that the shore was dangerously close. The breakers were pounding against the ship as the deck and the remaining rigging tilted toward the shore. Beyond the surf and a narrow beach, the land was covered with short green scrub and an occasional live oak tree. The leaves of the trees were being stripped by the intense wind but were clearly visible since the shore was now only yards from the distressed ship. The chests were pulled onto the deck and hoisted over to the boat. An ax and a spade were wedged under the ropes holding the chests. Oars were placed in the locks, and the two sailors and Johnny managed to climb down into the small craft. The yaw of the ship put the boat into the water without the crew lowering it, and it was released from the davits. Almost immediately, the boat jerked and spilled the cook out. He was immediately crushed between the boat and the hull of the ship. Next the wave's motion pushed the boat away from the grounded ship. The sailor tried to wrestle the oars to stabilize the boat. But the small vessel was at the mercy of the wind, and the oars proved useless.

The sailor pulled one of the oars from the lock to use as a pole to reach the bottom and steer the boat in the surf. As he leaned against the boat with all his weight, the surf pulled the boat in another direction, and the sailor was left holding onto the oar as his feet slipped off the rail of the boat. He slipped below the foamy surf, and Johnny never saw him again. Johnny was left alone in the boat. He held tight to the ropes lashing the trunks and tried to keep his feet wedged under a board. The next immense wave lifted the boat and carried it over the surf and into the lower branches of a big live oak.

The boat struck the oak and splintered. The trunks remained intact but scattered at the base of the tree. Johnny had been slung from the boat through the bare tree branches. He was battered, but otherwise intact. He noticed that even though the tree was stripped of its leaves, it was easily the biggest one along the shore. He looked back at the *Mirabelle* and saw that the wind was beginning to loosen boards from the deck and the hull. The ship looked close enough to touch but was likely more than fifty feet away. He saw Captain Mendoza on the deck, yelling something to him, but with the wind, he couldn't hear a word.

He found the spade and dug at the base of the tree. As he began to dig, he noticed the wind had died down. After he furiously dug a hole close to the tree trunk for the smaller chest, he began scooping sand over the larger chests. Suddenly, he could see the sun and realized that only faint puffs of wind were rustling the naked branches of the live oak.

The sudden stillness was broken by the sound of whistling. He looked into the bare branches of the oak and saw Bird sitting on a low branch, watching Johnny. He appeared undisturbed by the storm. His tune was "Swing Low, Sweet Chariot." It was the same song that they had whistled together on the plantation.

Above the whistle, Johnny heard Captain Mendoza. "Johnny, get the trunks covered, and I'll get over to you soon!" Oddly, he now heard the captain clearly in the still air.

Johnny resumed frantically digging and covering the chests. He took a moment to wave at the ship but was too out of breath from exertion to answer. Bird continued to perch on the oak branch and bobbed his head in time to the strokes of the shovel.

Johnny had the trunks almost totally covered when he felt a breeze from the west, the opposite direction from the ship. The brief sunshine began to be obscured. The rain that had suddenly stopped picked up again and now was coming in sheets. His attention was drawn to the west, and he could plainly see that he was on a narrow spit of land. Soon waves were lapping at the green brush and advancing. Now the wind was almost as forceful as before, but it was coming from the opposite direction.

Johnny looked back at the *Mirabelle* and noticed it was smaller. It was being pulled away from the shore. He saw the captain standing at the rail, yelling at him, but now the wind was deafening, and he couldn't catch a word.

He kept on scooping sand to cover the trunks as the water from the west came closer to him. Waves pushed their way over the land, and he finally gave up his task of covering the trunks so that he could climb to safety in the tree. As he climbed higher into the tree, he could see that the land was a narrow island. With waves lapping at his feet, he climbed higher. He looked about for the ship and saw it still being pushed back out to sea. He could barely make out the captain as he was frantically giving orders to his remaining crew.

Johnny climbed higher as the waves advanced and covered the land. Soon he was in the top branches of the oak. The tree was waving back and forth in the hurricane-force wind. Johnny wedged his small body between the branches and held on as best he could. Bird stayed perched on a top limb above the boy's head. "Now don't you be scairt, Bird," Johnny called up to him.

"Johnny don't want nobody to be afraid. Now don't you cry, Bird. Johnny don't allow no cryin'."

Johnny talked to the bird, and the bird stayed with his young friend. The water continued to rise. As the storm surge swept over the island, the two friends stayed together as they would always be—together.

Part 2

CHAPTER EIGHTEEN

On this sunny day, the shoreline was to the starboard as the sun began to settle over a vast expanse of water, lowering to a distant shoreline, miles to the west. The sloop's sails were furled, and the two-masted vessel lay against the lee side of the island. She was ready for duty, with the cannons charged and the crew anxious for action.

In the waning hours of the afternoon, Captain Benjamin watched for the *Queen Anne's Revenge* to appear in the setting sun. Benjamin was the swashbuckling young captain of a real fighting ship. He was lean and tanned with a tricornered hat, a black vest, thigh-high leather boots, and a bright red sash betraying his adventurous nature. A cutlass sharp enough to split a hair hung at his side. His first mate handed him his brass spyglass so that he could better view the horizon as he awaited the sight of the pirate's vessel. The first mate was fit, trim, and handsome in an outdoorsy manner. He had a short, full beard and long, gnarled tresses visible beneath a red headscarf. His frayed trousers ended at midcalf, displaying his muscular calves and bare feet.

The captain felt that Edward Teach, commonly called Blackbeard, would surely be entering the protected waters of the sound to avoid the British navy and to do battle with his sworn enemy, Captain Benjamin Triplett, and his crew. The first mate, J.J., was vigilant at his post as they scanned the horizon for the pirate whom they knew well from numerous previous encounters.

Captain Benjamin said to his faithful crew, "I know he will come, and when he does, we'll be ready. I can feel his treachery in my bones, and I can smell the aroma of his evil from here. I know he's coming."

First Mate J.J. echoed Captain Benjamin's words. "He's mean. I know he's coming too!"

The captain turned to the first mate. "Be ready for action. Unlike yesterday, this time we will give no quarter, nor will we accept it if offered, for that insane pirate Blackbeard would not be honorable enough to live up to any promise of mercy."

The first mate repeated the captain's message. "No quarters."

Over the last month, the crew of the *Good Ship Bogue Sound* had battled the dastardly pirates on a frequent basis, almost daily. They knew that today would be the day they would get the best of the worst pirate of them all.

....

"Momma says that supper's ready, and you'd better get in here and wash your hands better than you did at lunch if you want to eat tonight." The voice came from Kelsey, the sister of the two jaunty pirate hunters.

The spell was broken, and the *Good Ship Bogue Sound* instantly morphed into its original form: a discarded, leaky fishing boat that had long ago been beached on the shore of the sound by a forgotten storm and was too damaged and leaky for any redeeming use. She would never see open water again. Captain Benjamin's brass spyglass returned to the paper towel tube it was manufactured to be. His captain's attire changed into a T-shirt, shorts, and an old Atlanta Braves ball cap.

The intrepid Captain Benjamin answered his younger sister. "Okay. We're coming into port right now."

Kelsey responded, "And don't you and J.J. track any sand into the house, or I'll get blamed."

Benji was a fourteen-year-old with a vivid imagination and growing love for the sea and the lore of North Carolina's Outer Banks. First Mate J.J. was the four-year-old younger brother of

Benjamin and Kelsey. He adored his older brother and would follow him anywhere, even to the seven seas if he weren't only four. His headscarf that the boys had imagined to shelter long locks now covered a GI haircut. Instead of a beard, he had the soft, innocent face of a four-year-old. His uniform was his T-shirt and cutoff blue jeans.

"Can I get ice cream for supper?" asked J.J.

"We'll all get macaroni and cheese," said Kelsey. "But Mr. Bowen brought over a watermelon from his garden. You'll have to have that for dessert instead of ice cream since it was free." Kelsey, at seven years old, dreamed of being a ballerina and was still in her dance leotard from her afternoon dance class. The introduction to ballet was paid for by a grant from the local YMCA.

Their mother, Nan, was in the kitchen preparing supper when they all entered the house. "Now you boys get washed up. I know you've been in that nasty old boat all afternoon. I don't know why you boys want to spend your Friday afternoons dreaming about pirates when you could be fishing or getting some real exercise. There's plenty to do here at the house, and your dad and I could sure use some help."

The house did need a lot of work. The Triplett family had only recently moved to this isolated barrier island of North Carolina's Outer Banks. They had made the move not as tourists but rather out of economic necessity.

The Triplett parents had been employed in the inland piedmont area of North Carolina and had been prospering. The father, James, had a degree in textile engineering and had been running up the corporate ladder when the plant moved its production to China. James had been unable to find another position in the textile industry, the only option his company offered was to move to a different country and train the employee who would eventually take his job for half the salary. Unemployment barely paid the bills, even with the benefit of Nan's part-time job, so the Triplett family had moved on to plan B.

The Tripletts had a long history in coastal North Carolina. James's grandpa had been a commercial fisherman. He was a leather-skinned old salt who knew the toll that the sea took on a man's health and family, so he had urged his son, James's father, to make a life inland. James's father had taken jobs in construction in the booming economy of the fifties in the Raleigh area. His hard work paid off, and he was able to raise a family and see that his oldest son, James, got a college education. James's major in textiles was thought to be the basis for an occupation with great potential, but the family hadn't predicted the impact of the "global economy."

With James's unemployment benefits coming to an end, the family's savings were depleted, and their house inland had been on the verge of repossession.

Plan B was a radical move for the Tripletts. It consisted of a move back to the family's roots in the eastern North Carolina town of Triplett's Cove which had thrived in the nineteenth century as a fishing community. When the commercial fishing began to decline, rich northern duck hunters had discovered the bountiful estuaries of the sounds of the Carolina coast. Grandpa

Triplett hadn't gotten along with the fancy northerners. He harbored continued deep feelings going back to the so-called War of Northern Aggression and disliked the pretentious Yankees. He could have done better economically as a guide, but after becoming a widower, he continued the occupation of a commercial fisherman till the day he died.

His home, not much more than a boarded-up shack, had been vacant for years, but the land was unencumbered by any mortgage or lien. The house was situated pleasantly on the Bogue Sound with a pier that had been safe to walk on about twenty years previous. The lot was shaded by ancient live oak trees and faced the only road on the island. On the opposite side of the road there was a narrow strip of sea oats and dunes fronting the ocean. Some oceanfront homes were scattered along the beach where the elevation of that narrow ribbon of land allowed permits. Some adventurous souls accepted the risk of building a home on the ocean edge of a barrier island. James and Nan had made the decision to pack up the family's possessions in a U-Haul and move to the coast.

Benji had correctly identified their new home when he got his first view. "What a dump! Are we really going to live here?"

James had tried to put a good spin on the move. "It's not too bad. Give the place a little love and some elbow grease, and we'll be snug as a bug in a rug."

Benji retorted, "I know what you mean, but if there are any rugs in there, I'm pretty sure they have their own bugs already."

CHAPTER NINETEEN

The family had made the move in August, and Kelsey and Benji were soon registered in school. They were good kids and were able to adapt to almost every situation. But there were concerns about the kids and their new school. Kelsey was quiet regarding her new classmates. That was not a good sign for the usually bubbly seven-year-old.

Benji said, "They talk funny."

James knew what Benji meant. Known as Bankers, generations of residents of the Outer Banks of the Carolinas had been isolated until the roads improved after World War II. In the meantime, they had established their own version of language that had some similarities to Elizabethan English. James said to Benji, "So you think they talk funny. What do they say about the way you talk?"

Benji gave this some thought. "Well, they call me a prissy city boy, and sometimes I can't even understand them."

James tried to console the boy. "Benji, give it some time, and you'll make friends and get along."

Benji, the oldest and most honest of the kids, no matter how much it might hurt, replied, "I guess I have to get along since we're here on your plan B, and I don't think there is a plan C."

"Benji, do this for me. Make the best of it, and try to get along for the sake of our family. I'll make it up to you. I promise."

Apparently, word had gotten out that one of the Triplett families was returning home. From the time their U-Haul had turned in the driveway, cousins and neighbors had showed up to help make the old Triplett shack habitable. Tripletts, cousins of Tripletts, in-laws of Tripletts, and the whole population of Triplett's Cove (approximately one hundred) showed up to renovate the house.

James and Nan were at a loss for words when the entire community showed up to help them make the shack a home. They wondered what would make people do this. They asked several of the community workers why they pitched in. It was so different from living in Raleigh. The answer was always the same: "This is what we do."

Within a week the old shack could be termed a cozy cottage. During this time, James met his cousin, Mildred Triplett Cromer. Mildred worked at the local nursing home. She was very open and honest, as most Bankers (Banker referred to a resident of the outer banks barrier islands rather than someone associated with a financial institution) were. "I heard you lost your job in Raleigh. Are you workin' yet?"

"No, ma'am, but I'm open to anything I can do. I'll take about any job offered."

"If you're anything like your pappy and your grandpa, you can do about anything you want. Do you want a job?"

"Yep, I could use a job. What do you have in mind?"

Mildred responded, "At Sailor's Rest, we need a good facilities manager who can be an all-around fix-it man."

"Well, my degree is in textiles, but I learned a lot from my dad. He could fix nearly anything. I would like to try."

"Come by tomorrow, and meet our administrator. I think Sailor's Rest could use another Triplett."

One week later, James was donning a uniform of coveralls and doing maintenance at Sailor's Rest. He brought home manuals for the multiple systems to learn at night, and one evening, while looking over a book of nursing home regulations that was larger than the Raleigh phone book, a curious thing happened. He realized he was beginning to like his job. It had detail-oriented manuals and machines that were not terribly different from some of the systems in a textile mill. He would never move up the management ladder. He was the entire department.

CHAPTER TWENTY

Sailor's Rest, just a short drive from James's cottage, had a long history in Triplett's Cove, North Carolina. The long-term care facility had begun as a retirement home for retired sailors. The first Sailor's Rest in the New York area dated all the way back to 1801. Alexander Hamilton had written part of the initial deed. The need to accommodate retired seamen had filled the capacity of the northern facility, and another facility had been created on the Outer Banks of North Carolina. Over more than two centuries, the facilities had provided a more than comfortable home for aging, retired seamen. Being financially well endowed, Sailor's Rest offered rooms that were spacious and comfortable. The halls and common areas exhibited an array of expensive antiques and paintings with nautical themes that were the courtesy of a generous endowment.

Over the years, communications and the highway systems had improved, and sailors were able to have more shore time and more time to develop families. Subsequently, most of them had families to look after them in retirement. In the North Carolina facility, only a few retired seamen remained. As the census of retired seamen in the home declined, it had been opened to the regular population of the region.

The buildings had been regularly upgraded and replaced as needed over the years. James enjoyed the work of caring for the buildings and the physical plant with such a history. He enjoyed the odd moments he spent talking with the residents. They never lacked for stories to tell. Their only limitation was that they had very few people who would listen.

....

Dinner at the Triplett household was a regular family gathering. Even though the fare was not extravagant, it was substantial, and there was frequently seafood from neighbors and relatives, since the seas offered a variety of tasty additions for their meals.

Nan tried to keep the conversation going at the evening meal. In Raleigh it was called dinner. In Triplett's Cove, the evening meal was supper. She knew how difficult a transition to a new home and new friends could be.

Tonight's supper consisted of macaroni and cheese and fresh broiled bluefish donated by a neighbor, and it would be followed by fresh watermelon, sliced in the backyard and eaten on the back porch, with the family engaging in a seed-spitting contest that Benji would win.

Kelsey wanted to do an overnight with a friend from school over the weekend. James knew the family. They were distant cousins, and like about half of the village, they were also named Triplett. James remembered his father talking about the family, and they seemed to be good folks.

Benji devoured his mac and cheese and bluefish, as would be expected from a teenager going through a growth spurt. James asked him about school.

Between gulps, Benji answered in his usual teenage manner. "School's okay, I guess. But it's kind of boring. These kids just talk about fishing and their own sports. I guess I don't belong here."

James knew how difficult it could be for a teenager to be uprooted, so he wouldn't make a judgment on Benji's attitude, at least not now. "What about the fundraiser you had that flyer for? What's going on with that?"

Benji answered between bites. "Cans. They want us to collect cans to be sold for scrap metal to fund school projects. I've been

90

collecting ours, but we don't have many since you and Mom don't let us drink soda. I'm going to go up and down the road tomorrow and get some from the roadside and from the neighbors. They'll probably be happy to have me take out their trash and pick out the tin cans."

James said, "These days I imagine that most of the cans are aluminum rather than tin, but I don't think the scrapyard cares. Didn't the flyer say that the cans had to be in by Monday? Do you want me to help you go around to the neighbors' tomorrow afternoon? I'll get home from Sailor's Rest early tomorrow afternoon since it's the weekend."

"Nope. I'll clean out the roadsides, and I'll bet I get some big ol' bags of cans tomorrow, and maybe you can take me over to the school. They have a trailer they want to get full and take to the scrapyard."

"That sounds like a plan." James would have liked to talk to Benji more, but he felt lucky he could get that many words out of his moody teenager.

He turned back to his seven-year-old daughter, Kelsey. She was all bubbly and excited about a night away from home. This would be her first night away from the new house.

J.J., the Triplett's four-year-old, was a child who always seemed happy. James felt he needed to get in some conversation with J.J. just to keep him from feeling neglected, though he seemed content to enjoy his favorite meal. "What did you do today, Mr. J.J.?"

"I helped Ma till Benji and Kelsey got home. Then we went after that mean ol' black man."

"You mean you went after Blackbeard the pirate?"

"Captain Benjamin and me, we're goin' to get that mean ol' Blackbeard."

James teased his four-year-old. "You're taking to sea in that ol' leaky boat to chase the infamous pirate? Blackbeard did sail these waters. I hear that the local folks let him be as long as he behaved himself around here, but I guess you guys are not as charitable."

J.J. repeated words he had heard from Captain Benjamin: "He's a bad dude."

James could see that J.J. was keeping himself occupied, and his afternoons with Benji were giving Nan a chance to get some uninterrupted housework done. Things at their new home seemed to be going well.

CHAPTER TWENTY-ONE

Saturday morning in the Triplett household was almost like a normal workday. James was up at his usual time, and by six, he was sitting at the breakfast table with his morning coffee, toast, and scrambled egg. Benji was up early for a Saturday so that he could start collecting his cans for the school project. As they munched their toast and jelly, they listened to the radio for the morning news. After the obligatory news and weather at six, they listened to the *Dr. Bogus Show*. Dr. Bogus was a local legend. The word among the locals was that even the commercial fishermen listened to Dr. Bogus's advice on fishing. That was James's cue to get his coat and head to Sailor's Rest for his Saturday morning maintenance. "Now Benji, let's see how many garbage bags you can fill with those cans, and I'll help you bag them up and get them to the school when I get back. I should be back by early afternoon."

As James left the house for his truck, he looked in the dining room window and noticed that Benji had finished his breakfast but was still sitting at the dining room table, listening to the fishing stories on the radio. Dr. Bogus was giving his usual sage fishing advice. "It looks like we're in line to be the beneficiaries of the biggest bluefish run in decades. These fish won't be too choosy on their favorite bait. I've even seen them take a naked hook, but if I were a smart fisherman, I'd be looking at finding some nice juicy worms to feed those hungry bluefish…"

As the eight o'clock hour approached, Benji was in the woods behind the family's cottage with his spade in hand. He found a spot that was always in deep shade, with soft loamy earth. He began turning over the sandy soil in the hope of getting several cans of fishing worms. He intended to sell some during a walk down the beach since the surf fishermen always tried several kinds of bait. He had done this before and usually found fishermen willing to experiment with different types of bait till they found that magic combination. Then if he had any worms left, he would do some fishing for himself.

Soon J.J. came out the back door. A neighbor had taken Kelsey to the Y for her ballet class, and Mom was cleaning the house. J.J. was Benji's responsibility till he could be passed off to their mother's care. J.J. was usually a good kid, and Benji felt that he could be trusted to stay close to home.

J.J. waded in the water at the edge of the sound while Benji continued to dig for worms. He found some broken sand dollars and a few rusted cans for Benji. J.J. climbed into the old beached fishing boat and resumed his fantasy of being a pirate hunter. Up on the bank of the sound, only a short path from the shore, Benji was still using the spade to uncover his fishing worms while trying to keep one eye on J.J. at the same time. He noticed that J.J. was talking to someone, but he couldn't see anyone else down on the shore. The next time he dug his spade into the sandy worm-infested soil, he felt a metallic clunk. He bent down and found a hard chunk of shell or stone. He spat on the chunk and rubbed it clear of dirt. He had a rounded-smooth brownish stone. He thought it was unusual and sort of pretty. He dropped it in his pocket and headed down to the narrow beach to see who J.J. was talking to.

Benji looked around and saw no one. "Who was down here, J.J.?"

"I was talking to that kid. He don't talk much, and he sounds funny."

"What did he say?"

"He asked if there were any pirates in these parts."

"I told him, 'There had better not be any pirates around here. Me and Cap'n Benjamin, boy, we'll take care of them.'"

The boys were walking up the bank to the disturbed earth Benji had been turning over when they heard their dad's truck turning in the drive. Benji had no idea how the morning had passed so fast. The only cans he had collected were the few that J.J. had salvaged from the shore plus half a dozen coffee cans of worms.

J.J. ran to the truck and got a big hug as James locked the truck's door. James looked around and noticed an absence of any bags of cans. Next he looked at Benji, and as he gave him his hug, he mentioned that they had to talk.

After they got into the house and James and the boys had washed up, they went to the kitchen, where Nan was already making sandwiches for lunch and scooping out leftover watermelon for dessert.

After lunch, James took Benji aside. "Did you get any cans picked up for your school project?"

"I guess I forgot."

"Benji, how could you forget? That's the last thing we spoke about before I left for work this morning."

"Well, I listened to Dr. Bogus, and he said we should be getting some worms to be ready for the bluefish run tonight. I know I can sell some worms, and if we catch some fish, we may be able to sell them too."

"That's all good, but you promised to collect the cans for school, and you didn't. Benji, is this a pattern? I spoke with your teacher yesterday. She's concerned that you aren't giving school as much effort as you should. She knows you're smart, but she says you haven't been able to apply yourself. What do you think about that?"

"Dad, there's so much going through my head. I never thought of us as rich in Raleigh, but I didn't think we were poor either. Now we live in a shack. I know we're pinching pennies, and it's a lot to deal with. You used to be a boss, and now you're… you're just a janitor."

"I suppose you don't think custodial work is a necessary profession?" James actually was in charge of the nursing facility's many systems, but he had some cleaning duties as well. Benji would not appreciate that fine point at the moment.

"Dad, I really don't know what I think. I miss Raleigh. I want to like it here, and I don't want to make things worse for you and Mom. The kids talk funny. They talk about fishing and hunting, and they call me 'sissy' and 'citified' because I don't talk like a real Banker."

"Well, your teacher suggests you take on some project outside of school," said James. "And I don't mean just hunting and fishing. Let's take the afternoon to pick up as many cans as we can and add to the collection for the school. Then we can go over to the breakwater and see if we can sell some worms and land a few bluefish of our own."

After they had added three big bags of cans to the trailers sitting outside the school, Benji and James, with J.J. tagging along, headed over to the breakwater, where the outlet from the sound met the edge of the Gulf Stream. The fishermen were almost elbow-to-elbow. James and Benji took positions among the fishermen and saw a variety of bait on their hooks, including shrimp, cut mullet, and minnows. In the dusk, the ocean had a gray color, but along the north shore, there was a dark blue patch that seemed to be moving in the direction of the fishermen. Soon the fishermen began to get bites. Some fair-sized fish were hauled in.

But James and Benji had begun getting bites as soon as their worms touched the water. They were attracting attention from the surrounding fishermen, who inquired as to their bait. James pointed to the cans of worms, and the fishermen asked if they could buy some. James sold five cans of worms as quickly as he could pass them out, and Benji demonstrated his fishing skills. Even J.J. caught some fish, though Benji had to take them off the hook. Benji baited another hook for J.J. with a fat worm. J.J. almost cried when the worm was placed on the hook. But when the hook hit the water and was almost immediately dragged down by a big bluefish, the tears were forgotten, and Benji helped him reel in a giant fish.

James witnessed the brothers fishing together and could not help but comment. "Well, J.J., you're a real fisherman now. Once it gets in your blood, it'll be with you for life."

J.J. replied, "I hope I can fish for life, as long as Benji baits my hook."

Within an hour, they left the breakwater with a cooler full of fish and fifty dollars of worm money.

On the way back home, James decided to take advantage of their good spirits. He suggested that Benji begin coming to the nursing home on occasion to volunteer. He could see what James actually did, and he could talk with the residents. They always had interesting stories, and it might help both Benji and the long-term care residents. After all, what could happen?

CHAPTER TWENTY-TWO

The next Saturday morning, James and Benji were up before the rest of the family. James fixed eggs and toast for them both. Dr. Bogus's show was on the radio again. Fortunately, his show today was teaching preparations for future outings, rather than promoting immediate, urgent fishing opportunities.

James could tell that Benji was nervous about the new experience as they drove the short route to Sailor's Rest. The teenager took a small stone from his pocket and fretted with it in his fingers as one might do with a string of worry beads.

"Whatcha got there, Benji?"

He replied, "It's just a pebble I found on the bank when I was digging worms."

"Not too many rocks in the sandy soil."

On arrival at Sailor's Rest, James sent Benji off to meet his cousin Mildred. "Millie will show you around a little and give you a few chores and let you meet some of the residents."

Mildred Triplett Cromer was a long-time employee of the facility. She was a tall, thin woman with graying hair and ramrod-straight posture. Benji had heard from his dad that she was a no-nonsense person but would be fair if he tried his best as a volunteer.

Her sensible heels clicked across the hall. "Benjamin, your dad says you would like to volunteer at our facility—that maybe you'd like to see a little bit of what your dad does here and help out while getting to know some of our Sailor's Rest family. Yes,

I know they are residents in a care facility, but we treat each person as though they are aunts or uncles. Now follow me, and we'll do a little tour of the buildings."

First, they went through the halls of the skilled nursing facility. Mildred explained, "As we age, some parts of our bodies wear out before others. Residents in this section require assistance with several areas of their daily living. Some need intravenous fluids or antibiotics. They may need assistance with feeding or hygiene. A volunteer may be able to help them organize their personal space. Many like to be read to, but there are patients who will not even respond to the spoken word. They often are in need of company. The nurse can tell you which you may approach."

The next building was the assisted living facility, where the residents were not as debilitated. "They require some assistance with medication and some minor assistance with daily activities," said Mildred, "but they can take their meals in the dining room, and most can walk without assistance. These folks sure would enjoy someone to speak with. They don't get too many visitors, and a visit would go a long way to improving their lives."

The last building was the independent living section. It looked more like an apartment building on a campus than a nursing home. "Residents here can no longer live at home for a variety of reasons. Some even keep their cars, but most no longer drive. They can take their meals in the public area, or they have some cooking facilities in their apartments. Now let's look at the common areas." The dining area had linen tablecloths and chandeliers. The room was spotless and looked more like a space in a hotel than a nursing home. The next room had a hanging sign above the doorway that said "Bum Boat."

Benjamin asked, "What's a bum boat?"

Mildred answered, "When sailors entered a port, frequently they were required to stay on the ship. They were right there in the harbor and could see the city but were unable get into the town. Sometimes they had been on the ship for weeks, if not months. A bum boat was a boat that came around in the harbor to sell goods to the sailors who were unable to go ashore."

The room's brick walls were adorned with nautical paintings. Tables, some with inlaid checkerboards, and comfortable chairs filled the room. A figurehead of a lady with an ample bosom was prominently displayed, and on another wall a ship's wheel held a central position.

They finished up the visit with quick tours of the other areas, including the kitchen, the therapy areas, and the administrative offices.

Mildred continued, "Benjamin, you're fourteen years old, so we can't employ you, but you could be a big help to us if you'd be willing to volunteer. You can see what your dad does for us in maintenance, and you can visit the residents and talk to them. Many of our folks have very little family left and even fewer visitors. We're very proud of our facility and its history of providing care for our retired sailors. In the past, a career at sea was a very solitary lifestyle. The life of a seaman was essential to the country but left very little time for families, so when the time for retirement came, there were very few options. That's why places like Sailor's Rest were begun. But in recent years, most seamen have had access to modern communication and transportation and have been able to have families ashore. Mostly, they go elsewhere to retire to be close to their families. We have only a few retired sailors left, and most of our residents are from the surrounding communities. They still are in need of company. We'll have some chores for you, but if you have some spare time, visit the residents. Most of them have fascinating stories to tell."

Mildred introduced him to the staff on the floor and set him up with an aide in the assisted living area who would give him some work to do. Before leaving him with the aide, Mildred gave Benji one last tip. "You might want to be cautious when you talk to a few of our residents. Our remaining sailors are here partly because they haven't been able to adapt to normal society. So be careful around a few of our residents, especially Mr. Murphy."

100

CHAPTER TWENTY-THREE

Charles Murphy lived in the assisted living area of Sailor's Rest. He had entered the merchant marine profession at the age of eighteen to avoid a domestic situation. He had too many girlfriends and had made too many promises that he never intended to keep or had been incapable of keeping.

His years in the merchant marine had been filled with the adventures a young man craved. He had always found life to be a series of opportunities. As a mate in the merchant marines, he'd had a challenging career. Though most of his shipmates had family somewhere, he had a series of port-of-call romances but no permanent attachments. When the infirmities of age and arthritis had set in, he had had no family to fall back on. Sailor's Rest was a comfortable billet. He found the ambience of the place to be an ideal situation. Room, board, and health care were provided by the generous endowment that was now two hundred years old, and the female-to-male ratio was ten-to-one. Even better, the cost of staying at Sailor's Rest for non-merchant marines was expensive, so anyone else residing there was likely to be well heeled. Over the years of his stay, Charlie had romanced several of the residents. The staff knew of his proclivities and had tried to warn the ladies of his intentions as tactfully as they ethically could. But Charlie was so darned likable that the unattached or widowed female retirees were drawn to him like a magnet.

His current interest was Edith Alderman. Edith had been married to Albert, a hardworking insurance executive who had loved both her and his work. He had worked himself to an early death but left Edith with a sizable estate and a wonderful insurance benefit. She'd had household help at home, but her biggest problem was the loneliness. At Sailor's Rest, she found a private suite with all the amenities of home and the added benefit of companionship. She had her friends for bridge and even cocktails. She had regular dining companions in a well-appointed, well-maintained dining area with food comparable to that of most fine restaurants. And best of all, she had found Charlie.

....

Edith leaned in toward her friend Mable at breakfast. "That Charlie is so amusing," she said. "He told me about this pooch who stowed away aboard his ship in San Francisco. He cared for that puppy all the way around the world, including Singapore, Abu Dhabi, Naples, and Gibraltar. Then they crossed the Atlantic, passed through Panama, and finally sailed back to San Francisco, where he made sure it was adopted. Can you imagine how caring he was to that helpless dog?"

Mable responded, "He seems to be quite a fine gentleman."

Edith continued to gush, "And he's such a handsome man. Albert was handsome in an indoors-workaholic manner. That Charlie has the weathered complexion of a true outdoorsman. I find his full head of white hair attractive, and he's so vain about that little ponytail he wears. It's the cutest thing."

Mable leaned over the table and whispered in a very confidential manner, "Have you been affectionate with Charlie?"

Edith blushed. "Affectionate? Well, we've held hands watching the sunset over the bay. We've walked along the shore together, and I blabbered way too much about the grandchildren. I should have asked more about his life. He's seen and done so much more than I ever did."

Mable listened intently and responded, "I'll bet he's very experienced, if you know what I mean. Have you kissed?"

Edith leaned forward and whispered in a voice just audible above the clink of dishes and forks, "He kissed me on the cheek last evening when we sat on the swing outside my suite. I felt like I was sixteen again!"

Mable was a bit shocked by Edith's revelation, but she felt that as a good friend and the facility's resident busybody, she had a responsibility to espouse caution while also bursting Edith's bubble of happiness. "Edith, what if this Charlie is taking advantage of you? I suspect he has whispered sweet nothings into the ears of many ladies over the years. You may only be his latest conquest."

"Mable, I've thought of that, and I do suspect he is a man of *experience*, but I don't care. All I know is I'm the happiest I've been since Albert passed. No, I'm even happier than I was with Albert. Albert was comfortable and safe, but he lacked... well, he lacked passion. Charlie is boiling over with passion. And I'm as happy as I've ever been! And I'll tell you something else: I've got Charlie a little present." She reached into her purse and pulled out a velvet box. The box was royal blue with a white five-pointed crown on the top.

Mable gasped. "Is that what I think it is?"

Edith teased, "If you think it's a Rolex watch, you'd be correct. Albert had a thing about watches; he had too many. I don't think he would mind my giving a little present to Charlie. He's been such an angel."

Mable again responded more somberly. "Edith, I hope you know what you're doing. You know what they say, 'there's no fool like an old fool.' You'd better be careful, or you might get hurt."

Edith seemed taken aback by Mable's warning. "I may be hurt, but I've been hurt before. I may be an old fool, but I've been foolish before. And I can tell you, Mable, that I've been in love before, but love is where you find it, and if I can find it again, I'll take a chance."

CHAPTER TWENTY-FOUR

Charlie sat in the snack area, named the Bum Boat Lounge, and sipped a root beer while spreading a game of solitaire on the table before him. Life was looking up for a man who had learned to live comfortably by his wits. Edith had just presented him with one of Albert's Rolex watches. He had feigned reluctance about accepting the extravagant gift but finally had been persuaded to take it on his condition that he put it away and not wear it in public for the time being. When they were able to more formally announce their affections, he would gladly don the expensive watch.

As he continued his solitaire, Eddie, one of the long-term facility janitors, approached him. Eddie had been pretending to sweep the hall, but he had kept more than a casual eye on the couple as Edith successfully persuaded Charlie to accept the token of their friendship. "Man, what is it with you? You no more than finished fleecing that old Smith gal before her family came and took her up north, and now you got your eyes on another pigeon."

Charlie looked up at the janitor. "Jettie Smith was a charming lady, but at ninety, she was, I must admit, a bit old for me. However, my time spent being affectionate with her was not wasted. She wrote several large checks to me before her family got wise, stopped payment, and moved her out of state. You know, I'll miss the old gal."

"You mean that you'll miss the money."

"Eddie, Eddie, Eddie, you underestimate me. I had sincere feelings for Miss Jettie. And neither her family nor the administrator could prove any illegality. I can assure you that my billet is very secure. You know, there are only two of us retired seamen here, and old Sam Dodger is well past ninety-five. Do you know what happens if there are no retired sailors in residence?"

From the blank expression on Eddie's face, Charlie knew that explanation was needed. "With no retired seamen present, the facility loses part if not all of the endowment they have enjoyed since 1801. I guess they'll put up with a few extracurricular activities by old Charlie. And old Charlie will continue to enjoy the company of the legions of white-haired beauties who come through here as long as they have adequate bank accounts." As Charlie said this, he developed a slight leer that revealed his true character.

"Eddie, there's no harm here," he continued. "I provide the affection they miss because their loved ones have passed on or didn't care, and they provide me with a few luxuries to aid me in my old age. All in all, it's a fair proposition."

Eddie could only shake his head in admiration. "I've got to give it to you, man—you're one slick dude." He resumed his sweeping in the corridor and left Charlie to his solitaire.

As Charlie was puzzling on which card to place, he spied a child wandering the halls in sneakers, jeans, and a T-shirt. What was unusual was that the child had an ID tag marked "Volunteer."

"Young man, come here. Yes, you. Don't be shy. I won't bite. That is, I won't bite before supper."

The boy was passing out mail and magazines and seemed reluctant to come into the snack room.

"Come on in, Master... What's your name?" quizzed Charlie.

"Benjamin, Benjamin Triplett."

"Master Benjamin Triplett, what crime did you commit to have to spend your Saturday here with us old gomers?"

Normally outgoing, Benjamin now felt shy, and as he answered, his voice seemed tremulous and girlie. "I shucked off a school project to go fishin'. Dad works here and thought I needed to see what he does here and what the home is like."

"So, your old man wants to have a 'take your pup to work' day. What do you think about our humble home so far? Come on and sit down for a minute. No one here gets mail that can't wait a few minutes. You can humor an old sailor in his dotage. After all, the only people I talk to here at Sailor's Rest remember the Alamo from seeing newspaper accounts, so a conversation with a young person is a breath of fresh air."

Benji sat down ramrod-stiff on the edge of his chair, the same posture he had maintained in the principal's office. He wondered if this was the Charles Murphy that Cousin Mildred had warned him about.

"Tell me about your family, young Triplett. With a name like Triplett, they likely came from here. The woods are thick with Tripletts in these parts, but you don't seem to have that Banker's accent."

"My great-grandpa grew up here, but Grandpa moved to Raleigh. Dad studied textiles in college and worked in a mill till it moved to China, so here we are, back where the Tripletts started." As Benji told his story, he sensed his palms sweating, so he felt the stone in his pocket and gripped it tight.

The adolescent amused Charlie. He wondered why the young man was so nervous. "I'll tell you what, young Master Triplett, come and see me occasionally, and I'll tell you stories about the mariner's life. It'll grow hair on your chest and make you want to take to the high seas."

This excited Benji. No adult had ever spoken to him in this manner. "I'd like that. Are you Mr. Murphy?"

"Yes. I'll bet you were told about me, weren't you?"

"I was, well, warned that you were…"

"Different. I'll bet they said to stay away from me because I'm different, didn't they?"

"They didn't say that exactly, but I think that may be what they meant."

"Well, when you come here to volunteer, you ask for Old Murphy, the merchant marine, and you and I will be buddies."

"Do you know any pirate stories?"

"Do I know any pirate stories? I know more about pirates than you've got time to listen. I can tell you all about pirates from yesteryear and even some modern pirates. They might simply be stories, but some of them just may be true. What's true, and what's not true? I'll let you be the judge."

CHAPTER TWENTY-FIVE

That evening the Tripletts gathered at the table for dinner and a review of the day's activities. Nan laid out a meal of fresh boiled shrimp with a salad. There was also sweet iced tea, the universal drink of the South, along with fresh ripe cantaloupe for dessert.

After they said a simple grace, the family's accounts of their day began. Nan had completed her Saturday ritual of straightening the house. The kids were getting better at putting their things away after the downsizing move, but they still could be messy. Nan recounted the conversation she'd had with their neighbors about the new fishing trawler at the wharf, and then Kelsey felt it was her turn. She had met new friends on the beach and discovered that they were cousins. In Triplett's Cove, it was difficult to find families that weren't related in some fashion.

James asked, "Benji, how was your day?"

Benji's response was typical of a fourteen-year-old. "You know how my day was. You were there. I swept the floor, emptied trash cans, and straightened the magazines in the Bum Boat." After that statement, he had to explain to his siblings and mom how the residents' lounge had gotten its name. Then he mentioned that he had visited with some of the residents.

James asked, "Who did you visit?"

"Well, the main one was Mr. Murphy."

"Didn't Mildred ask you to avoid him?"

"I know she mentioned it, but he's an old man with a lot of sea stories. I kinda like talking to him. He's been all over the world and seen a lot more than Raleigh and Triplett's Cove. He told me that he could tell me some real goochy pirate stories that would curl my hair."

James's interest was piqued. "Mr. Murphy has a reputation. I don't think you can take anything he says as true."

"Aw, Dad, I know that, but I think they're still good stories. If I go back, I'll just listen. I don't have anything I could tell him anyhow."

Even J.J. was eager to show off his day's activities. After he swallowed the last shrimp on his plate, he took another sip of iced tea and began whistling. The whistle was not quite a tune, and it wasn't loud, but it was definitely a whistle.

After the short concert, a surprised James asked, "Who taught you to whistle?" He looked around the table, and Nan, Benji, and Kelsey all shook their heads no—it wasn't one of them.

J.J. looked very proud that he had a secret. He waited till everyone was paying close attention and then said he had a friend down at the "noise" who had taught him.

Benji asked, "What noise are you talking about, and who is this friend?"

Kelsey piped in, "He calls the sound 'noise.' Sound, noise—do you get it?" Then she punched Benji on the shoulder.

After a moment, Benji said, "Well then, who is this friend?"

J.J. responded, "He's Johnny."

James hadn't known there were any other children who lived close. He asked, "Did you say that you played with Johnny down at the sound?"

J.J. seemed annoyed that his family was having problems understanding him. "Yep, down by the noise I play with Johnny, and he teached me to whistle."

James asked, "What does Johnny look like?"

"He looks a little like Caleb." Caleb was one of J.J.'s play-school friends from Raleigh. He was one of the few African American children in the play school.

"Does he live around here?" Nan asked.

"I think he lives in the trees, him and his bird."

"I'm sure that he lives somewhere with his family," Nan responded.

Kelsey chimed in again. "What kind of bird is it?"

"It's a big red bird. He whistles, too." J.J. wondered why everyone was so interested in his new friend. He and his bird were merely playmates. J.J. was already reaching over to get a section of the sweet, juicy cantaloupe.

James and Nan gave each other knowing looks. They were familiar with imaginary friends. Both Benji and Kelsey had gone through periods when they had their own special friends that no one else could see. J.J. must have picked up the whistle on his own. Since the move had been hard on the whole family and an imaginary friend was likely a benign passing phase, they felt it was probably a healthy adaptive behavior.

CHAPTER TWENTY-SIX

Back at Sailor's Rest, Murphy had finished his evening meal and was playing cards in the Bum Boat with his cronies. Across the table sat Mel, a retired storekeeper who had been at the home almost as long as Murphy. He was one of the few residents whom Murphy would occasionally trust with a secret. Mel looked about to be sure that no one was in earshot and then looked over at Murphy above his cards and mused, "Is sweet old Edith still under your spell?"

Murphy grimaced at Mel's comment and replied in a hushed voice, "Keep your voice down—we don't want everyone to hear my business. And yes, I can say with some confidence that Edith and I may now be considered an item. Today she presented me with one of her late Albert's watches, a fine Rolex. That's a much better item than could ever be found in your shop."

Ordinarily, Mel would be insulted by the insinuation that his shop had carried inferior goods, but he had to admit that his inventory had never included the Rolex brand. "So, Murphy, are nuptials pending?"

Murphy laughed so loud he almost choked on his after-dinner coffee. "No, Mel, I firmly intend to stay free and single, but if Edith finds it in her heart to contribute to the welfare of a poor and ailing fellow senior citizen, who am I to decline her wishes?"

"Murph, you're as fit as a fiddle. You haven't even had a cold in years."

"Mel, time and tide wait for no man. Who's to say what will happen to our health at any time? And if Edith gets the impression that I'm having a health issue, who am I to dissuade her from that impression? Now close your trap. Here comes Edith now."

Edith was at the door and used her cane to totter over to the card table. Murphy stood and held out a chair for her. "Edith, please join us," he said.

She sat carefully, as though she feared that even a sudden move would crack her fragile spine.

Murphy sat back in his chair. "Mel and I were finishing up the last hand of our card game, weren't we?"

Mel took his cue. "Nice to see you, Edith. Will you excuse me? I promised my daughter I would call her this evening, and time is passing."

As Mel stood, Murphy began to cough. The cough expanded to a spasm. Murphy covered his mouth and nose with a napkin as though there might be some horrible corruption he was hiding in the cloth.

Edith took the notice that he'd hoped she would. "Murphy, are you okay?"

"Edith, I've developed this cough I can't seem to clear. I hate to mention this, but I've begun to lose weight, and I'm coughing up more colorful stuff and even an occasional streak of blood."

"Charles, you must see a specialist. What does our doctor here say?"

"He says I need tests and scans and some expensive therapies that my insurance doesn't cover. Don't worry about me. I'll be fine."

"Nonetheless, I am worried. Now you find out how much you'd need to have to pay for those tests, and let me know."

"Edith, I couldn't impose on you. You've been such a kind friend…"

"Tut-tut—that's what good friends are for, and we are good friends, aren't we, Charles?"

"You're far too kind to an old man, Edith."

"Well, you just get yourself well. My, look at the hour. I must be getting to my room for my evening toddy. I do enjoy my little cordial."

....

The next morning in Mildred's office, James took a short coffee break. She asked how Nan was adapting to island life, how the family was adjusting, and whether the school was working out well for Benji and Kelsey.

James seemed positive. "Nan is becoming a real Banker. She's learning the island cooking and getting into the culture. School was a little bumpy for Benji at first. He still spends a lot of time in that old beached, leaky fishing boat over at our place. He and J.J. like to imagine they are hunting Blackbeard aboard a ship of the line, but now he seems to be making friends, and he loves fishing. His favorite show is not on MTV, but an early morning radio show, *Dr. Bogus*. He even enjoys his time here at Sailor's Rest. I thought it would be a punishment for him, but he enjoys it. Kelsey is our little princess. She is involved with dance classes at the Y, and school has not been too much of a transition for her. We can't thank you enough for the way all the cousins helped us get settled."

Mildred seemed pleased with the family's transition and then asked, "What about little J.J.?"

"J.J. is a champ. We had some concerns when he began talking about a playmate at supper the other night. We figured out it was an imaginary friend when he described him as a little black boy. We don't have any close black neighbors. He's even learned to whistle. He says that his imaginary friend, Johnny, taught him to whistle."

This caught Mildred's attention. "Did you say that J.J. has an imaginary black playmate?"

"Yep, Nan thinks it's kind of cute. She reminded me that both Benji and Kelsey went through a phase of imaginary friends when they were about that same age, and they grew out of it in a few months."

113

Mildred replied, "I guess you don't remember the stories. I suppose your dad didn't tell you much about the local myths."

"What stories?"

"Over the years, for as long as the Tripletts have been settled on the Banks, there have been stories about a little whistling boy who is black. He seems to appear in the treetops, usually during a storm with gale-force winds."

"Are you getting ready to tell me a ghost story? Our move has been traumatic enough, but with my family's active imaginations, I don't need for them to be talking about spooks and goblins."

"I'm only giving you the history. Tripletts have been making a living fishing here since settling before the Civil War. Mostly, they were subsistence farmers and fishermen, barely making it from year to year, but they loved the independence. And on occasion, when a ship grounded on the shoals, they would do their best to rescue the souls aboard those ships, but they also considered their cargoes the bounty of the seas. There was a time, not too long ago, when every house in the cove had some timbers that had come from the ocean rather than the mainland.

"Anyway, every generation or so, stories come up about the little whistler boy. Once the story gets started and someone looks up into the high branches of a tree and sees or senses a little black boy, then a wind picks up, and someone else hears a whistling in the trees that sounds like a melody and remembers the story of the little black whistler. My opinion is that it is a lot of imagination mixed with a legend so old that no one can remember the origin."

James found this fascinating. "But J.J. doesn't know anything about myths or legends. No one has even mentioned to us that the cove could be haunted."

"I told you it was just a story."

CHAPTER TWENTY-SEVEN

In Triplett's Cove, the only nightlife was centered on fishing. Closer to home, there were no streetlights and only rare headlights passing. The Triplett family was a cheery group in the evening.

Outside their home, the breeze kept the needles of the scrubby pines and the waxy leaves of the live oaks moving. The sounds of the surf and the breeze mixed with an occasional rustle in the brush from birds and animals, created a special ambience. It was very different from the Raleigh area.

But the Tripletts were not the only ones adjusting. High in the pines, there was another adjustment occurring. Johnny and Bird were aware of new activity. Mendoza's last command had been to bury the chests and await his return. Johnny and Bird had been faithful to that request. Johnny was aware that he had passed to a new existence. He had no hunger or pain, and time was a concept that had faded from his memory.

He remembered the terrible storm and the island being totally covered with water. He remembered clinging to the branches as the rising water took his breath. But time since then had been a fickle thing. The next two hundred years had meant little to Johnny. Each day the sun rose, and the birds played, fished, and nested. The mullet jumped in the sound. He and Bird communed with each other through their whistles. Time seemed to have some rhythm only when there was activity, especially when children generated the activity. Most humans and animals could not see him, though a few could occasionally sense his presence. The current residents of his thicket included a child who actually saw him. He saw Bird as well. Now, with a child present, Johnny sensed the profound loneliness of the guard duty commanded by Captain Mendoza. The encounter with the child called J.J. by his family excited his spirit.

....

After school on a warm autumn day, Benji and J.J. were at their favorite pastime. The beached boat was once again the object of their fantasy. "First Mate J.J., how is the weather?"

J.J. dutifully answered his hero, Captain Benjamin. "Captain, we have fair weather and a following sea."

"Excellent, mate. Any sightings on the horizon?"

"There's a barge on the waterway."

Using his paper-towel tube as a telescope, Benji looked toward the barge, loaded with some unknown bulk cargo, being pushed down the inland waterway by a tug. "Aye, matey, I spy her. She's fully loaded, moving slow. You've had no luck finding any pirates?"

"No, sir, Captain. I see no pirates around here."

"First Mate, we need more crew. Where is Kelsey?"

J.J. reported, "She's at her dance class."

"Mate, we need more crew if we're going to be a match for Blackbeard."

J.J. asked, "What about Johnny? I'll bet he would like to be a pirate hunter."

Benji had heard his parents talk about J.J.'s imaginary friend, and he vaguely remembered that he'd had a secret friend when he was a kid like J.J. He grinned at his young mate, and in the spirit of playing along with him, he said, "Bring your friend along; he's welcome to join the crew."

"Aye, Captain, he'll come aboard in a minute. Can he bring his bird along?"

"What kind of bird?"

"I dunno. He's a whistling bird. He's red and green. He might be a parrot."

"Well, every ship needs a parrot. Didn't you see *Treasure Island*?"

J.J. looked to a thicket of trees on the shore a few feet away and called, "Johnny, do you want to play pirate hunter? Bird can come." J.J. seemed to listen for a moment and then said, "Captain Benjamin already said it's okay." J.J. looked back at Benji with a satisfied smile.

Benji asked, "What was that?"

"He's coming down from the tree. He'll be here in a minute. Didn't you hear him?"

"J.J., I don't see or hear him. I don't think he's real."

"He's real all right. And if you can't see him, that just makes him more real. That makes him real special." With that, J.J. reached to the shore side of the boat and made a motion as though he was helping his friend over the gunwale and into the boat. He turned to Benji and reported, "Seaman Johnny and his bird are aboard, sir. Ready to cast off." He indicated that Johnny was there beside him on the bench seat and that the bird was perched on the bow.

Benji played along as though he could see Johnny, and J.J. assured him that Johnny was obeying his orders. Soon J.J. began to whistle. The tune was "Swing Low, Sweet Chariot."

Benji asked, "Where'd you hear that?"

J.J. replied, "Can't you hear Bird? That's one of his favorite tunes."

CHAPTER TWENTY-EIGHT

The next Saturday morning, Benji and James were again at the nursing home. James routinely did several hours of duty to be sure all the systems at the facility were working, and Benji found that volunteering a few hours every other Saturday morning was not too painful. He didn't openly acknowledge that he actually enjoyed the time with his dad and with the residents. The small tasks he performed were greatly appreciated, and he actually found himself listening to the stories the residents told. He especially looked forward to Charlie Murphy's stories. This was the same Murphy he had been warned to stay away from.

On this day, he once again found Murphy in the Bum Boat Lounge. "Well, young Master Benjamin. Are you coming around today to hear more sea stories? If so, you'd better be wearin' a seat belt because these stories would knock you out of your seat."

....

"Well, young Benjamin, let's start by talking about your history of Bankers. What a bunch of hypocrites you Bankers are." Charlie Murphy seemed to be in the mood to present a lecture, and Benji was, for the moment, a willing and enthusiastic student.

"There were lifesaving stations up and down the Outer Banks, especially where the shifting shoals had claimed ships for hundreds of years, but many Bankers were also known to the seagoing population as wreckers."

Benji asked, "Why were they called wreckers?"

"Well, Benjamin, the folks living on the Outer Banks were there for a reason. Mostly, they enjoyed their independence and the isolation, but it was a lonely life that depended on the bounty of the sea to provide. Even then, they were mostly poor and lived at a subsistence level. When a ship would wreck on the shoals or be washed up by a storm, the Bankers saw it as a boon. Their reputation was that they tried to save the lives of the passengers and crew of disabled ships, but they were also known to strip a ship of everything valuable down to and including the ship's timbers. You're familiar with Nag's Head, just a little north of here?"

"Sure, Dad took us up there on a vacation," Benji replied.

"Do you know how it got its name?" Murphy asked.

"Is it shaped like a horse's head?"

"That would be simple, but before the age of airplanes and satellite imaging, it was difficult to see that the shape looked like an animal. One theory, and I think one that is far more likely, is that the Bankers encouraged shipwrecks and gave the place that name before the lighthouses were ever built.

They would hobble a horse on the beach where the shoals were the most unstable and tie a lantern around its neck. Without lighthouses, a ship's crew rounding Cape Hatteras would be keeping a sharp lookout for any sign of danger. Watching for a light bobbing up and down near shore, a crew could easily mistake the hobbled nag for a ship at anchor, moored in calm waters. Their mistake would often lead to a grounded ship that was fair game for the wreckers of the Outer Banks and a bonus to the subsistence fishermen. And you know, Benjamin, those were your ancestors."

Benji was surprised at Murphy's assumption. "How do you know those were my family?"

"Because, young Master Benjamin, your last name is Triplett, is it not? The name Triplett is almost as old as these barrier islands. I have seen that name on many a list of pirates. I seem to remember that one of Blackbeard's mates was a Triplett. Now, you're not a pirate in disguise, are you?"

"No, sir, we're not pirates."

"Well, Benjamin, we never know what we'll be in any given circumstance."

Murphy continued schooling the adolescent. "Now let's talk about real pirates. You'd think that the golden age of piracy was over when Blackbeard was slayed in 1718. Well, piracy was going strong long before and has kept going since then."

Benji really wanted to hear more of the pirate stories spun by Mr. Murphy, but he was becoming wary of the man he had been warned to avoid. He absentmindedly took the stone from his pocket and began nervously manipulating it in his hand.

Living by his wits for years had made Charlie more observant than the usual resident, and he noticed the odd-looking stone young Benjamin fiddled with in his nervous hands. "What is it you have there, young fellow?"

Benji responded, "Nothing. Just an old rock I found while digging fishing worms behind the house."

"May I see that trinket?" Charlie asked.

Benji reluctantly handed over his souvenir. A little voice was screaming at him that he should leave, but he wanted to hear more of the stories.

Charlie took the small stone and examined it. "Do you have any more of these?"

"There are a few more rocks there, but it's so sandy where we live; it's mostly just sand and shells."

Charlie looked at the stone closely. He held it a few inches from his eye. He took his glasses off and used them as a magnifier to closely observe every detail of the trinket. Then he spun it on the tabletop. He drew it across the flat surface as though he was expecting it to make a mark on the table. Finally, he gave the stone back to Benji and asked, "Did you say that there were more of these stone the same size?"

"Well, I guess there are other ones. I saw some more when I was digging, but they weren't just on the ground, and there were a few clumps of them. They were like shells clumped together."

Charlie looked away as though his trivial interest had lapsed. "Well, it's mildly interesting, Master Triplett. Now would you like to hear about a real mystery of the Outer Banks?"

"Sure, I would. I've got time." Benji was hooked, and Charlie knew he had an entranced audience.

Charlie began his next story. "Following the Revolutionary War, the former colonies had an uneasy peace with Great Britain. You heard all this in school, Benjamin. Do they still teach history in school?"

Benji said, "I've heard of the XYZ Affair."

"Well, did you hear about American ships being boarded on the high seas by British ships and American seamen being illegally impressed into the Brits' navy?"

Benji nodded in the affirmative.

"Well, the American navy was nonexistent. To counter the British and with the likelihood of another war on the horizon, the United States government granted letters of marque to establish privateers. This enabled ships to more or less skirt the law, and it was legal under the Constitution of the United States.

There was a privateer ship called the *Patriot* that had been successful under a letter of marque. She had been refitted as a merchant ship and left Georgetown on December 30, 1812, bound for New York. Among her passengers was twenty-nine-year-old Theodosia Burr Alston. She was the daughter of the notable though defamed Aaron Burr. That made her the equivalent of a present-day superstar. In addition, she was the wife of the governor of South Carolina.

The ship never arrived in New York. There had been a notable storm off Cape Hatteras that accounted for the loss of several ships, including the HMS *Margery* and the merchant/privateer *Mirabelle*. Theodosia's father, Aaron Burr, and her husband, Governor John Alston, mounted searches in every seaport from New York to Nassau, but inexplicably, they did not search the Outer Banks around Hatteras."

Benji had listened transfixed. "What happened to the ship?"

"She was presumed lost at sea, but there is more to the story. In 1833, there was a deathbed statement from a dying Alabaman who reported that he had been part of the crew that had captured the *Patriot*, robbed it of anything of value, and murdered all passengers and crew.

Then in 1848, there was another dying confession from a purported privateer crew member who said there was an Odessa Burr Alston on the captured ship who had chosen death over submission to the captors. Finally, in 1869, in our own Nag's Head, a portrait was found in a poor sick lady's home. A doctor attending her got the story that a ship had been discovered ashore two miles south of Nags Head at the time the *Patriot* was lost. The sails were set, the rudder was lashed, and everything was intact in the cabins, including vases of waxed flowers, silk gowns, and a portrait of a gentlewoman, which now graced the wall in the old lady's home. The doctor accepted the portrait as payment for his services, and eventually, word of the portrait reached Theodosia's family in New York. Finally, in 1888, relatives of Theodosia viewed the portrait and reported there was a remarkable family resemblance."

Murphy paused and asked, "Could you follow all of that, Master Benjamin? Well, if you have some doubts, you can see and hear more about the loss of the *Patriot* at the *Graveyard of the Atlantic Maritime Museum* in Hattaras. They even have a fine reproduction of the portrait of Theodosia Burr Alston."

Benji asked, "What actually happened to the *Patriot*?"

Murphy said, "Wait, there's more. Around the time the doctor was treating the old lady, a novel was published that was promoted as being partly true, partly fiction. In the book, Dominique Youx, the half-brother of famous pirate Jean Lafitte, the hero of the Battle of New Orleans, is said to have confessed to capturing the *Patriot* and murdering Ms. Theodosia Alston. What's the true story? The seas keep their secrets, and rarely do we find the truth."

Benji had already spent more time with Murphy than he had intended, but he had one more question before he left. "Are there still pirates today?"

Murphy laughed. "Young Benjamin, we're much too civilized for that sort of thing now. Besides, why should the lawless spend their time on the dangerous oceans, risking life and limb, when there are such lucrative ventures by safer means?"

Benji looked puzzled.

Murphy continued, "Now our pirates wear expensive suits and ties and wing-tip shoes. They call themselves lawyers or insurance executives and swindle clients and companies and get richer than any pirate ever anticipated. Now don't you forget that, Benjamin."

Benji knew he wouldn't forget this afternoon, but suddenly, he couldn't wait to get out of the room. He said, "Thank you, Mr. Murphy. I've got to go, but I'll be back for more stories." He said this so excitedly that he accidentally reverted to his high girlie voice and could have kicked himself for it.

As Benji was leaving the lounge, Murphy called out with one last comment. "Master Benjamin, I'd be interested in seeing any more of those curious rocks. You know, they're sort of an oddity, and I love a good mystery."

Murphy was still in the Bum Boat Lounge as his confidant Eddie came in and sat with him. Murphy mused, "That boy doesn't know that the lucky charm he's carrying in his pocket is either a silver piece of eight, or a real Spanish doubloon. I can't be one hundred percent sure since it's encrusted with centuries of calcium, but it's much more than a lucky stone. I'll wager that where he found that one, there's likely a treasure trove. You know, Eddie, what I see here is a grand opportunity. Master Triplett's lucky stone is exactly that: lucky for us. I may have to demonstrate to Master Benjamin that modern pirates do, in fact, exist."

CHAPTER TWENTY-NINE

On a lazy fall day, the Triplett kids were enjoying one of those ideal afternoons that occur before the onset of winter. On this occasion, they were all three lying on the narrow beach bordering the sound (what J.J. still occasionally called the "noise"), gazing at the fluffy clouds lazily crossing the sky as the sun-warmed water lapped gently over their bare feet.

Kelsey asked Benji, "What do you see in the clouds?"

Benji's imagination led him in a nautical direction. "I see a ship. It's one of those we see in the Viking movies with a large square sail, and it even has a dragon on the bow. Don't you see it?"

Kelsey responded with the extreme certainty she always exhibited. "There are *no* sailing ships anywhere in the sky, you goof, but I do see a magical elephant crossing over that cell tower on the mainland shore. It's one of those East Indian elephants with bells and a raja sitting on its back. I see it very clearly. J.J., you do see it, don't you?"

J.J. responded, "I sorta see an elephant, but I think it looks like Marmaduke."

Benji laughed. "What's a Marmaduke?"

J.J. answered, "Mama reads me the funnies every morning, and I see Marmaduke every day, and that cloud is Marmaduke. Now let me ask Johnny what he sees."

Kelsey looked around. "Who's Johnny?"

Benji answered, "Johnny is J.J.'s *special* friend." He gave Kelsey a big wink.

J.J. looked into the trees that were only a few feet away, so close they were almost hanging over the sound. "Johnny, what do you see in the clouds?" After a minute, J.J. reported, "He says they look like cotton fields to him."

Benji exclaimed, "Where is Johnny? I don't see anyone!"

J.J. indignantly replied, "He's sitting right there in that big oak tree. I can see him making a face at you right now. And there is his big red bird perched a foot over his head."

Benji said, "I'm sorry, J.J. I can't see him, and I'm looking right at—"

Kelsey interrupted Benji, shouting, "I see him! I see him! I thought he was imaginary, but he's right there. His pants are frayed, and his shirt is ragged, and he's barefoot like us. And I see his bird. I see a great big parrot. My gosh! He's a beautiful parrot with bright red plumage and a green body and some yellow on his tail. Will they come down here and play with us?"

Benji said, "I still don't see them. Are you making this up?"

Kelsey almost seemed mad. "Why can't you see them? They're right there! You're a big dummy!"

Benji didn't take this as an insult since it came from his little sister. "Go ahead, J.J. Have Johnny come down here, and let's play."

J.J. said, "He's shaking his head no. He'll play with me, but I don't think he wants to come down now. I think he may be too shy to come down with all of us. Maybe he'll come down later."

....

Back at Sailor's Rest, Murphy was firming up his scheme with the orderly, Eddie.

"So, Murphy, are we digging for treasure or mining the fortunes of the white-haired ladies?"

Murphy was calmly sitting in the lounge, sipping the malt beverage he had managed to procure though it was against his "doctor's orders." He had actually spent his fictitious medical visit time in a nearby bar to pad the timeline of his story. "I intend to do both. The boy doesn't know that he has a Spanish doubloon or a piece of eight. I don't know if he has found a treasure or a random coin from someone's pocket. I planted the idea in his head that there are all sorts of pirate mysteries surrounding the Banks, so if I make a good story, we may be able to follow him along to see if he has stumbled on a treasure. I think we can play him like a fiddle. But we are close to a payday with that old gal Edith, and I think she can afford to supplement my pension. I'm guessing that the Rolex she gave me is worth at least five thousand dollars, and I intend to triple that before her daughter shuts her purse. I tell you. I've got her eating out of my hand. Now pass me some of those mints. I can't have sweet old Edith getting a whiff of a brewed beverage on my breath. She's got to believe that her beau is ailing."

After disposing of his empty beverage and using a handful of mints, Murphy was ready for his rendezvous with Edith. As he expected, she appeared at his customary table in the Bum Boat Lounge after the evening meal and before it was time for her evening toddy.

He acted, as usual with Edith, ever the gentleman. He stood, and after a slight bow, he pulled out a chair for her. He made it a point to stay in a stooped position and to wince slightly and rub his left flank as he attended to the formality of greeting her.

Before Edith had an opportunity to ask, he inquired about her well-being. "How was your day, Edith? Did anything notable occur at our humble residence while I was absent today?"

Edith had obviously noticed Murphy's discomfort and was certain to inquire about his health, but there was plenty of time to work his magic. She reported, "Ms. Evans went to the hospital with a hypertensive event, and Mr. Garfield's grandson came for a surprise birthday celebration. He's so handsome, and he brought the great-grandchildren. They are so cute. They make a really good-looking family. Now tell me, how was your doctor's visit?"

"You know these doctors. They can never make up their minds. They always want more tests and more visits and more needles—and of course, more money. But I can't complain. My pension and insurance will hold me for a while, but if this thing draws out much longer, I may have to look at going elsewhere for lodging. And the pain in my side is getting anything but better."

Edith seemed genuinely concerned. "Murphy, I thought that you were seeing this doctor for your bad cough."

Murphy was momentarily taken aback. He had for a moment confused the symptoms he had catalogued for Edith's story. "Well, he says that my cough and the pain in my side are connected. He thinks that there is fluid around my lung that is causing some increasing pain in my back and side. Some sort of rheumatism is causing the fluid to collect and make me cough."

Edith patted his hand and answered, "I don't want you to worry about finances, and I certainly don't want you to consider moving elsewhere—that is, unless you are dissatisfied with your accommodations…" She let that simmer for a moment and then added, "Or unless you're dissatisfied with your fellow residents."

Murphy had been making facial expressions that were a combination of painful winces and game smiles indicating that he was enduring discomfort with a sense of good humor, but when Edith suggested that he might be dissatisfied with the company he kept, he had to respond. "Edith, how could I be upset with anything you do? You are a breath of fresh air to this old sea dog. I only wish that we had more time together." With that comment he gripped his side more firmly and even let out a slight but distinct groan.

She tenderly took his hand in both of hers. "Murphy, I may be a bit older than you, probably several years older, but I'm going to be around for a long time yet. Our whole family lived to be grand old dames."

He responded, "I appreciate that, love, but I was speaking of myself. I fear that my voyage is close to its final port."

Edith seemed even more concerned. "We'll keep positive thoughts, and please, Murphy, let me know if there is anything, and I do mean *anything*, I can do."

He rose from the table with some apparent discomfort and helped her gain her balance as she rose from her chair. They walked hand-in-hand down the corridor to her suite. He gave her a gentle kiss on the cheek as he wished her a good night.

On the way back to his room, Murphy looked like a new man. He walked with a new spring in his step, as though he had not a care in the world.

CHAPTER THIRTY

Back at the Triplett household, dinner consisted of clam chowder with fresh cornbread and sides of sweet potatoes slathered in butter and pickled beets donated from Cousin Mildred's pantry.

Dinner conversation at the Triplett table was more animated than usual. James asked Nan how things were going.

"The tribe is all hyped up about J.J.'s new *friend*," she said. "Somehow, his imaginary friend is now Kelsey's playmate too. Seems like a regular *folie à deux*, imaginary friend of two."

James said, "Are we sure that this Johnny is imaginary and not a real, breathing little boy?"

Benji answered, "Well, I can't see him, and I looked hard. Mom looked, and she couldn't see him either."

Kelsey interjected, "Well, I saw him, and I saw his beautiful bird, too. And I'm not imagining it. He's a real little boy, and he has a real bird!"

James looked at the one at the table with the most experience with their mystery boy. "Well, J.J., what did you see?"

"I saw Johnny when we were lying on the noise beach, but when Mom came down, Johnny left."

Nan looked at James. "Should we start setting an extra place at dinner?"

James replied. "I don't know, but at least he seems to be friendly."

....

After dinner, Benji began to think about his recent visit with Mr. Murphy. He remembered how interested he had been in the lucky charm stone. Benji pulled it out of his pocket and looked at it more closely than he had before. He had always been attracted to the smooth surface of the stone, but now he noticed for the first time that there were some areas of irregularity. There were ridges on the stone. They had been worn by the scrubbing of sand and wind but could still be felt. When he shone a flashlight on it from several angles, he could almost see a form. Perhaps it was a figure eight. Benji now suspected that this was not just a pretty natural stone.

Since it was not yet dark, he took his old worm shovel and headed back to the area beneath the big live oak tree. He scraped away the leaves and weeds from the surface and began to dig. He easily found the worms he was looking for, as Dr. Bogus had previously directed. As usual, he found more now than when he was ready to go fishing. He fetched a can and put them in with a bit of sand. There was no use in wasting them. Next he began turning over spades of dirt, making a circle at the base of the tree where he had dug previously. He found several more of the single stones. It still seemed curious that he didn't see similar stones anywhere else around. He had dug for worms elsewhere and had not seen any such stones. Except for sand and shells and roots, he hadn't seen anything at all. He had even helped dig a ditch for a neighbor lady, and he had encountered only sand and roots. No stones.

When he had completed a circle one spade deep and about three feet in diameter, he began to dig a little deeper. By then it was getting late, and he knew that he would have to go in and do his homework soon. He had dug out several shovels full going two spades deep when he thought he had hit a root. He looked down and saw that the wood he had uncovered was straight rather than rounded like a root. It looked old and was rotting. He dug around the piece of wood and found some rusted metal around one end of the wood.

Nan yelled from the window, "Benji, you'd better get in here! This math homework won't do itself."

Benji thought about this. There were any number of reasons a rotted piece of wood would be there. After all, his favorite pastime was playing on an old beached fishing boat that was nothing but mold and soft wood. He smoothed the ground he had disturbed with his shovel, covered up the stones with one final scoop and picked up his fishing worms and shovel to take back to the house. As he was cleaning up the ground, he thought he heard wings flapping in the top of the oak. He looked up, but in the waning light he couldn't make out anything. He felt a little spooked, so he covered the disturbed earth with more leaves and weeds. He was almost up the walkway to the house when he again thought he heard a bird. Shorebirds were all around, and some could be heard day or night. Finally, he thought to himself that there was no way, no way at all that could be a parrot.

CHAPTER THIRTY-ONE

At Sailor's Rest, Charles Murphy was asked to visit the front office. Administrators of retirement facilities had to balance a fine line between pleasing the residents and pleasing their families. Seldom were both easy to satisfy. They frequently wanted completely different things. The administrator also had to keep the facility on its budget and hopefully show at least a small profit. Even with a generous endowment, Sailor's Rest was not immune to financial issues. It had a long and esteemed history, and the buildings and campus were frequently renovated and well maintained. The staff was competent and generally motivated since otherwise the only alternative was work related to the fishing industry. This administrator, Captain Adam Smith, was a retired navy veteran and could spot a con a mile away, but knowing and proving were different.

Captain Smith had known Murphy and his reputation for some time. As Murphy reclined in Smith's office, they both knew the reason for the visit.

Smith began the conversation. "Charlie, how long have you been at Sailor's Rest—is it six or seven years?"

"I've been here five years since my back gave out and I had to give up my berth."

"Really? It seems longer," Smith said. "Have you been happy here? I mean, have we met your needs?"

Charlie responded, "I've been happy here. It's not perfect; no place is, but I can smell the salt air and feel the breeze off the bay. I hear the surf when the tide comes in. And you run a tight ship, so an old salt like me couldn't ask for any better."

Smith pressed on. "How is your social life?"

Charlie laughed out loud. "Do you think I'm looking for female companionship? I'm a bit old for a sexual liaison, but you've got to admit that with a ten-to-one female-to-male ratio, there is opportunity for female companionship."

Smith decided to go directly to the reason for the visit. "Charlie, you do have a history with the ladies of our facility. You do remember Emily."

Charlie slicked back the hair to his white ponytail that now went halfway down his back. "Emily, now there was a real lady. She was so lonely. I think she really valued the companionship that we shared while she was here."

"Just how much did she value your companionship?"

"Smith, are you suggesting that I was a kept man? Perhaps you think that I was some sort of a gigolo."

"Emily's daughter thought so. Her mother held her own power of attorney at that time, and they still haven't figured out the amount of the checks she made out to you."

"Well, she was competent—then. Her daughter engineered her finding of incompetency after she moved to another facility."

"Her daughter was really steamed at you, at us, at the facility in general. She threatened legal action, but since her mother was legally competent, there was little that could be done."

Murphy responded, "Her husband had passed away shortly before she came to Sailor's Rest and had been her constant companion for sixty years. She deserved to have a close friend."

"You mean she deserved to have a close friend like you? How many 'close friends' do you think you've had in your time here at our facility?"

"I've probably had a special companionship with four ladies," Charlie said, counting only the elderly ladies that he assumed Smith knew of. There were several others that he had mined like a vein of gold, but there was no point in bringing up those associations unless the administrator knew specifics.

133

Now Smith wanted to discuss Charlie's current conquest. "Tell me about you and Miss Edith."

"Well, you know, a gentleman never tells, but I will confide in you that Edith is a victim of a marriage with a husband who lived for his work and put it first and his family, including his wife, second. She soaks up even small courtesies like a sponge."

"Charlie, her daughter has been here. She has some concerns. She admits that Edith's attitude is improved, and she gives us—us meaning mostly you—credit for making Edith's transition to widowhood smoother. The daughter says that she seems content, but she is worried that you may be taking advantage of her."

"Look, Edith's not insane, and if she wants to make me a bit more comfortable, what am I to do?"

"Charlie, I don't want to talk about evicting you. But we do have a reputation to uphold. Now perhaps you could focus your affections on other residents. You may need more friends than only Edith."

"Adam, you know that you need me. Even if Edith has resources, I'm still more valuable to you because my residency here keeps your endowment. Now, you know I'm a one-woman man—or I should say, one-woman-at-a-time man."

The administrator had to admit that Murphy, as one of the few remaining retired sailors in residence, was important to the facility's endowment. And even if the reputation of the facility was at stake, who was he to deprive a single, elderly, mentally competent lady of a relationship? "Okay, you've made your point, but your behaviors don't endear you to the families or to your administrator."

"I'm just a simple sailor, no more, no less." With that Murphy left the room. As he walked back to his room, he began to suspect that he needed to shorten his timetable for completing his affair with Edith.

....

The next morning was Benji's volunteer Saturday morning. He completed his chores, delivered the mail, filled the water

134

pitchers, and helped his dad with several tasks. As noon approached, before his dad took him home, he made his visit to Murphy.

As usual on a late Saturday morning, Murphy was sitting in the Bum Boat Lounge with a deck of cards and a cup of coffee. He looked up and saw Benji. "Well, Master Benjamin, have you come to chew the fat with the old man today?"

Benji was puzzled. "Chew the fat? What does that mean?"

"To parlay, pass the peace pipe, or just have a friendly repartee between friends. What's on your mind today, my friend?"

"I thought you might have some new sea stories for me."

"I suppose you want to hear more stories. What if I told you a story of cemeteries? That's right. This is a story about graveyards. These are north of Hatteras and on Ocracoke Island."

Benji asked, "Is this still about pirates?"

"Well, there are pirates, and there are opportunists. Sometimes it's hard to tell the difference."

Benji didn't understand all of what Murphy was saying, but he was sucked into the conversation.

"We've talked about the hazardous seas and treacherous shoals around the Outer Banks. You'll remember that the area was called the Graveyard of the Atlantic."

Benji did remember some of this. "You told me about the *Patriot* ship and the governor's wife."

"That's right, young Benjamin. And did I tell you that every coastal community had a lifesaving station that employed several locals and that those communities all had what was called wreck commissioners or insurance agents? Roads were treacherous or nonexistent in those days, but in Buxton, a road was built just for salvaged goods and dismantled beached ships. Now, were those good people, your Banker ancestors, just scraping by and making a living? Were they heroes for saving countless lives, or were they taking advantage of the misfortune of others? Were they pirates or saints?"

Benji wrinkled his brow as he wrapped his brain around the

puzzle. "Well, I guess they took advantage of others' misfortune, but they didn't cause their problems. They helped."

"What do you think about the ship owners who lost their investments?"

"I guess that anytime you deal with the ocean, that is a chance you're taking. That's why they have insurance." That was the best answer Benji could suggest.

Murphy smiled and grasped his hands above his head in a motion of triumph. "Exactly so, young Master Benjamin. Then let me get back to my original point. During World War I, lone German submarines harassed ships off the Outer Banks. The subs were a nuisance, but they did not seriously deter shipping. But in World War II, the U-boats began patrolling in packs, refined their tactics, and were much more effective. From late 1941 to 1942, a record number of ships were lost, mostly due to German torpedoes. In a period of ninety days in 1942, fifty large ships were sunk by U-boats, and the ruts of the Buxton road got deeper and deeper as the pockets of the locals got fuller and fuller. One such ship sunk was the British merchant ship *San Delfino* in April of 1942. A few days after the sinking, the body of an unknown British sailor washed ashore in Buxton and was buried there. In May of that year, a British trawler, HMT *Bedfordeshire*, that had been commissioned to do anti-submarine tactics was torpedoed and sunk with all hands. Some days later, the bodies of four British seamen washed ashore in Ocracoke and were buried there with honors. Within a week, a fifth body, another sailor from the torpedoed trawler, washed up in Buxton. He was interred beside his countryman. Those small cemeteries are regular tourist attractions, and annual ceremonies honor the victims.

Now, Benjamin, should the Bankers who became prosperous due to the war be able to build fine houses or in many cases move inland due to profits from salvage? Should they give it all back, or are they simply beneficiaries taking the spoils of war?"

"I guess I don't think they should give it back. They were at war."

"But we were at war with the Germans, not the poor sods that got a torpedo up their... well, they were torpedoed. Let's agree that sometimes the space between right and wrong can be a bit gray and not black or white."

Benji was not sure he agreed but ended up saying, "Yes, I guess so. But I've got something to show you."

Benji reached in his backpack and pulled out a dark stick of wood about eighteen inches long. It was blackened with age, and the once-smooth surface was now coarse and rough where the grain had deteriorated due to aging. On one end of the piece of wood, there was a rusted metal bracket, and a sliver of metal still protruded through the bracket. Benji said, "I found this under the tree where I found my lucky stone."

Murphy took the sample of wood and examined it closely. He held it to his nose and whiffed as though it was giving off some distinct aroma. He pressed his thumbnail into the wood to test its firmness. Then he surprised Benji when he stuck his tongue to it and tasted it. Finally, after his close examination, he asked, "Benjamin, did you find anything else?"

"I found a few more stones. Here, I brought you a couple. I guessed that you could use a little luck too."

Murphy took the stones and examined them nearly as carefully as he had the stick. He put the stones aside and asked, "Did you find any more wood or metal parts?"

"Nope, I just dug up that stick."

"Well, thank you so much for the good-luck charms. I'm sure they will bring us great luck and fortune. I can't make much of the wood, but if you have any more discoveries, be sure and share them with me."

"Yes, sir, I'll let you know whatever I find."

"Good boy. Now be off with you, you scurvy pirate!" Murphy said with a big grin on his face.

Shortly after Benji left, Eddie showed up at Murphy's table. "Well, you spun quite a tale for that Triplett boy. Are you working some angle on the boy or his dad? You know, his dad seems to be a pretty good fellow."

"Well, Eddie, we live in difficult times. We must look after ourselves before we tend to the welfare of others. Besides, the elder Triplett has a steady job. He'll never miss what he doesn't know he has."

"You have some more information on the coin—uh, stone— young Benjamin carries in his pocket, his lucky charm?"

"The boy brought in a piece of wood he found along with the coins. He didn't know its significance, so he brought it to me. The wood was old, real old. And the metal was wrought iron fixed with hand-hewn nails. I think it was a hasp from a chest. From the size of the hasp, it must have been a large chest.

Apparently, there are several *stones* there. They are undoubtedly Spanish coins of precious metal, and our goal, Eddie, is to take possession of the contents of that old chest. So, Eddie, are you in?"

CHAPTER THIRTY-TWO

As Eddie manned his mop on his way down the hall, he could not wipe the smile from his face. The news that a fortune of unknown amount would likely be his to share with Old Murphy was enough to make him smile and put a spring in his step. Later that afternoon, he vacuumed the corridor of the private suites, an area called the Gold Coast by the staff. As he passed Edith's suite, he noted that the door was ajar, and he could hear loud voices from somewhere inside the suite. Eddie was not beyond gleaning a bit of information on a resident, especially one that Murphy had picked out as his pigeon.

"Mother, how could you give Daddy's Rolex to that… That watch was his pride and joy. You do know how much he scrimped and saved to get his first Rolex."

"Amy, I know how many nights I spent at home raising you children mostly by myself while Albert had to see just one more client. There was always one more client. And Amy, I know he loved his Rolexes, probably more than he loved me, so if I want to give one of his precious watches—which **is** my watch now—to a dear friend, I will do so. And Mr. Murphy is nothing like your father. He tells me stories of his travels to every port in the world. And boy, has he ever had some experiences." As Edith said this, she sat down and fanned herself, as though remembering the racy tales of Charlie Murphy that had almost been too exciting. "He is the opposite of your father, and you know, there may be snow on

139

the roof," she said, pointing to her own hair, "but he still has fire in the furnace."

"Mother, have you lost your mind? I don't think I'm talking to my mother who wouldn't let me go out in the snow to play without a complete snowsuit and bundled up so much I could hardly walk."

Edith responded, "Well, maybe I am a little crazy. But I'm head over heels in love, and if I'm insane, I can tell you that it's a wonderful feeling. I don't want to be normal. And if I decide to give Mr. Murphy a lot more than a watch, well, this may be my one true love to share my personal feelings and desires, my wealth, and my remaining years with. And did you hear me when I said 'my wealth'?"

Amy stood in the middle of the Edith's living room with her mouth gaping open at Edith's statement of love for that broken-down Charlie Murphy, who looked more like a reprobate than the refined gentleman her father had been. "Well, if that's the way you really feel, I may need to take legal action to protect you and your assets. I've already spoken with Captain Smith, the administrator, regarding your over-generous gifts to this Murphy. I'll be in touch with our attorney as soon as possible to see if I can get control of your finances to protect you from yourself. Mother, I really think it's in your best interest."

Edith now raised her voice more than Eddie had ever heard. He would not have thought that she could yell so loudly. He was not immune to eavesdropping, but he would have needed to be deaf to miss this fracas.

Edith did not hold anything back as she unloaded on Amy. "You just try to have me declared incompetent! I'll pass any test those doctors and lawyers can cook up. And I'll tell you something else: I may have made some bad decisions in my life, but if I have, it was staying with a man who could provide me security but lacked passion. Now Murphy—there's a man who exudes passion, something that Albert, your daddy, totally lacked."

Eddie eased down the hall with his vacuum cleaner, still turned off. He pretended to be adjusting it so that he could continue monitoring the conversation. After a minute or two, Amy slammed Edith's door shut and stormed out of the facility. Eddie couldn't wait to give this intelligence to Murphy. The old man had already been warned about Edith's family, but now the daughter was sincerely concerned about Murphy's actions regarding Edith.

....

As Benji rode home with James that afternoon, he described his visit with Mr. Murphy. He asked, "Did our ancestors really rob those people that came aground on the shoals?"

"Benji, the lifesaving stations saved more lives than could be counted. Those men would take a small boat out to a distressed ship in the teeth of a hurricane, with no expectation that they would return alive. And keep in mind that this was before health insurance and benefits. These men were staking their lives without any support for their families if they drowned on a rescue. As you know, Bankers take care of each other. That was the only insurance they felt they needed."

"What would the Bankers do if their livelihood depended on the sea?"

"They made a meager living when times were good, but they literally starved when times were bad. Then a ship loaded with a valuable cargo might run aground. It was no one's fault, and almost all of these cargoes and ships were insured. Certainly, the Bankers took the cargo for salvage and frequently took apart the ship if possible. Back then, many Bankers' houses included building materials from salvaged ships. It was a way of life."

Benji thought about this for a long moment. "I guess life was hard for our grandparents. I'm glad we live now instead of back then."

James had a different slant. "They had the sea, and they were closer to nature and family than we are. They felt lucky to be on the Banks, and you know, Benji, I'm liking the Banks myself."

Benji agreed, "I'm beginning to like it here. And I think that Kelsey and J.J. like it here too."

....

That evening after supper, the family was watching the local news. They heard all the news of fishing tournaments and local high school football scores from Friday evening, and finally, the weather report came on. Once again, a mild late fall was continuing. Apparently, winter would be late this year and hopefully mild. Near the end of the forecast, the weatherperson said, "Now look over here at the west coast of Africa in the Cape Verde Peninsula. We see the beginning of a tropical wave that developed over the last twenty-four hours. Now this is not yet a concern, but we do need to keep an eye on this. It's late in the season for tropical storms, but they are unpredictable. Here at the weather center we'll keep you updated if this develops into anything."

Usually, Nan barely noticed the weather report. She was usually clearing the table and beginning to wash dishes and put the leftovers away, though with a teenage son there were few of those. She had remarked to James in the last few days that here in the center of hurricane season, there had been very little talk of hurricanes and very little stormy weather. She had heard the ladies talk about shopping and stocking up on supplies in case of a "big blow," but she had not yet stocked up on storm supplies for their family. While they were doing better here, James's check from the nursing home didn't allow for any contingency plans. Nan had paid attention to the weather report as she cleared the kitchen. After the report she asked James what they should do to prepare for a possible storm. Thinking back to the weather report, Nan wondered if the broadcaster intentionally avoided the word, hurricane.

"This old house has withstood storms since my grandfather built it. If the storm is severe, we can drive back to Raleigh. We can stay with your relatives there till we can return. If we don't need to evacuate, we should stock up on some canned food, candles, and flashlight batteries and store up some water to last as long as a week. You know, we just got that emergency radio.

Remember, if the weather gets bad, I've got responsibilities at the nursing home. I would likely need to go over there to help with the generator, and if they need to evacuate to the mainland, well, I'll need to help with that. If we get to that point, I'll want you to take the family across the bridge, and I'll meet up with you all on the mainland.

But that's enough talk of storms. Let's have a plan, but pray we don't have to use it. Now let's talk about the kids. Benji actually looks forward to his mornings volunteering at the home now. He gets his head filled with all sorts of sea talk by a retired merchant marine."

Nan wrinkled her brow. "Isn't that the man that Mildred said he should stay away from?"

James responded, "I think Mildred overstated her warning. Now Murphy sure is a colorful character, with his long white hair and incredible stories, but he's well past being harmful. He does have an eye for the ladies, but I can't see that there is any harm in Benji listening to his stories. Some are entertaining, and others are outlandish."

After discussing Benji, there was a pause in their conversation that was rare in the Triplett house. Things seemed unusually quiet. James asked, "Where are Kelsey and J. J. this evening?" Kelsey and J.J. had made themselves scarce after supper.

Nan answered, "Kelsey got her homework done early, and now she and J.J. are down on the beach playing with Johnny and Bird."

"Now wait a minute. We do know that J.J.'s friend is imaginary, don't we? Do we need to be setting that extra place for dinner that we joked about—or putting out some birdseed just in case we have guests?"

Nan looked amused. "The way J.J. talks, you'd think he is real, and Kelsey has been tricked into believing she sees Johnny and his bird as well, but he only interacts with J.J. No, I don't think we need to set a place for him and his bird, but if you don't see any harm in Benji's elderly playmate, Murphy, then I don't think that J.J.'s friend is a danger either. Deal?"

James did have a confession for Nan. "Cousin Mildred says that J.J. may not be the only one to see the little black boy. She says that he has appeared before, years before. He seems to appear in times of storms, but he's never harmed anyone."

Nan thought that that might explain a lot. "Then either J.J. is acquainted with an apparition, or he is living a fantasy after hearing myths from long time Bankers. J.J. seems to be thriving, but we'll keep a close watch for ghosts and imaginary friends alike."

"Okay, it's a deal. We'll also keep a close watch on the weather till the hurricane season has officially passed, and we'll both try not to worry about our children's imaginary and real-life friends."

CHAPTER THIRTY-THREE

Monday morning found Administrator Smith in his office, looking out his large plate-glass window eastward to the bay. He had been watching the weather reports as well, considering it part of his job to be on top of any weather situation. So far, the hurricane season had been mild on the North Carolina coast, with storms hitting in other areas of the country but so far sparing coastal Carolina. The tropical wave mentioned in the weekend weather report was likely just another cautious observation, but he would be ready in any event.

Murphy had no concerns regarding the weather; he was more concerned with the status of his latest conquest. He was sitting in his usual chair in the Bum Boat Lounge while the orderly Eddie gave him the latest news.

"I'm telling you, Murph, Edith's daughter has no use for you. She was giving Edith *down the country* about her boyfriend. Edith thinks you're the best thing since sliced bread, but Amy thinks you're a geriatric gold digger."

Murphy only smiled at this. "I must say, I do resent being called geriatric. As for being a gold digger, time will tell. I haven't struck gold yet, but there is always hope, Eddie boy. Lord knows that I've mined for that gold as hard as possible. I can only hope that I'll soon strike it rich."

Eddie smiled at Murphy's comments, but at the same time he wanted to give a warning. "I hope you do strike it rich, and I hope you share the riches with your old friend and confidant Eddie.

My luck usually flows in the opposite direction. Why, if my ship ever came in, I'd likely be found at the train station waiting on it. But I'm tellin' you the truth: Edith's daughter plans to get control of her finances so that she can't give you anything else. I'll bet she's seeing a lawyer today."

....

The Triplett household continued through that week, rocking along in its predictably chaotic way, much as any family with three active children and financial pressures. On that Thursday, J.J. overslept. He was usually the first one up, tugging at Nan or James's covers and raring to get his day started before or with the sunrise. But on this day, Nan had to go to his bed and roust him out.

He said in a feeble voice, "I don't feel good, Mommy."

Nan checked his fever under his arm and found it to be 101 degrees. Her experience with two older children kept her from feeling alarmed. She was sure that it was a twenty-four-hour virus.

She gave him fever meds that should help with his fever and achiness, but at lunch, Nan checked his temperature again and found it had increased to 104 degrees in spite of the recommended dose of acetaminophen. Now J.J. had that weak look in his eyes—they were beginning to appear sunken, and all he wanted to do was sleep. She called their family doctor, who agreed it was likely a virus but suggested she take J.J. to the emergency room just to be checked out.

The closest hospital was over on the mainland, and the traffic was maddeningly slow. Nan called James, who reported he would be home when Benji and Kelsey returned from school. He'd check with Nan then, and she would certainly call when she had any news about J.J.

The emergency department was as chaotic as Nan had feared. Adults and children of all ages were sitting and waiting to be escorted back to the treatment area. The nurses called it "triage." Nan was ready to make a scene in the reception area to ensure that J.J. got evaluated when a nurse walked by and saw how ill J.J. looked. She immediately turned around and went back through the emergency department doors, returning in seconds with a J.J.–sized wheelchair. She got him back into the treatment area and had him hastily seen by a doctor. Nan could tell that the nurse was concerned that this illness was more than a simple virus.

The doctor thoroughly examined J.J. and looked ever more concerned as he continued. Finally, he addressed Nan. "Mrs. Triplett, I don't know exactly what's wrong with J.J. He may have a simple virus as you suspected, but it could be something more serious. Has he had any exposure to ticks?"

Nan tried to remember. "He spends a lot of time outside, and he gets plenty of bites, but we haven't found any ticks."

The doctor continued, "Has he had any recent episodes of illness, or have there been any changes in his behavior?"

Nan said, "Till today he has been his usual playful self. He is almost always smiling. He has developed an imaginary friend. He calls him Johnny."

The doctor asked, "How does this friend manifest itself to J.J.?"

"Oh, he's convinced that Johnny is a neighborhood child. He even has a pet parrot. We've checked, and there is no Johnny or pet parrot, but we can't convince J.J. We've even considered setting a place for Johnny at the table."

The doctor smiled. "Imaginary friends are common in children J.J.'s age. I doubt there is anything more to that, but it could be a sign of a more severe or prolonged illness. I'd like to do some further tests since we don't yet have a reason for J.J.'s fever."

Nan became even more concerned. "What kind of tests?"

The doctor said, "Most of these are routine. We'll get a chest x-ray and some blood tests and check his urine for infection, and I think it would be prudent to do a lumbar puncture."

"Doctor, that doesn't sound routine. You're beginning to make me think this might be serious."

147

"Well, Mrs. Triplett, it may yet be a simple virus, but let's do some tests and try to find out what J.J. is dealing with."

Nan called James. "You'd better get over here. J.J.'s fever is not going down, and he looks real sick. They're talking about a lot of tests, including a spinal tap."

Two hours later, with James and Nan present, J.J. had not improved. He was still listless, he had a sunken look in his eyes, and his fever was still high enough that it worried the nurses.

The doctor returned with news. "J.J. still has that worrisome fever, and his white blood cell count is elevated. Other than that, his tests look relatively good. We suspect he has a middle ear infection; we call that otitis media. But right now, he's a sick little fellow. I want to get him into the hospital and start some intravenous fluids and antibiotics. We'll keep a close watch on J.J. I'll bet that he'll be better in the morning."

But the next morning, J.J. was no better. Nan and James had taken turns sitting with him and never left his side. Their extended Triplett family had pitched in to watch Benji and Kelsey. The nurses had continued medication for fever and discomfort. The intravenous fluids and antibiotics continued.

On Saturday afternoon, James was sitting with J.J. when the child aroused. He sat up in the bed and looked around and began talking. "Yes, this is a good place. You've never seen a room like this?"

James thought that J.J. was delirious due to his fever. But J.J. was entertaining his visitor. He saw Johnny at the foot of his bed. Bird was there as well.

Johnny said, "No, I never seen no place like this."

"I'm sick. I think they call this a hospital. I've never been to a place like this either. I'm sure glad to see you—and Bird, too."

"Yo' windows don't open. Where you get the wind from?"

"Air comes out of that thing under the window."

James looked at his son in confusion. "J.J., who are you talking to?"

J.J. looked at the foot of his bed rather than his dad and said, "I'm talking to Johnny and Bird. Don't you see them? They're right there."

He continued to jabber with Johnny and Bird while James stabbed at the call button. He didn't know what was happening, but he knew he didn't like it. The nurse came in and rechecked J.J.'s temperature and found that it was still over 104.

The doctor came and reexamined the child. "There doesn't appear to be anything new. We'll recheck a blood test to see if there are any changes."

The test showed that J.J.'s white blood cell count was now practically normal. But his fever was still high, and though he was more alert, he was enthralled with his imaginary friends. The doctor said, "We often see this. Children who have severe illnesses frequently use their imaginations to develop a friend to help them cope. I'm confident that this Johnny and his bird are a temporary manifestation. When J.J. improves, they will likely go away."

James said, "They seem real to J.J."

The doctor said, "They can evoke strong feelings. It's better to let them go for now."

The next twenty-four hours passed with no change. James took Benji and Kelsey to the community church on Sunday morning while Nan stayed with J.J. At Sunday school, Kelsey prayed as hard as she could for the recovery of her little brother. She squeezed her eyes tightly shut as she mouthed her silent prayer. Benji did much the same, but as a teenager, he was not about to show his emotions.

During the preaching, J.J. was added to the prayer list, so he got the support of the entire congregation. Following a prayer for healing, the next song was old and familiar:

Spirit of the living God; fall fresh on me.
Spirit of the living God; fall fresh on me.
Melt me, mold me, fill me, use me.
Spirit of the living God; fall fresh on me.

After the service, James took the children to the hospital to see if they would be allowed to visit J.J. When they reached the hospital, both Kelsey and Benji felt the place was "way too creepy." They were waved through to J.J.'s room, and to their surprise, there was J.J. sitting up in bed, watching cartoons.

Nan shared the news that his temperature had normalized, and he was feeling better, but now he had a rash. Looking at J.J.'s arms and legs, James saw that they were now covered by a red, lacy rash.

Nan reported that the doctor had just been in and seemed happy with J.J.'s progress and would be back again soon so that he could talk to James and Nan together. She had no more than gotten those words out of her mouth than the doctor arrived.

"Roseola!" exclaimed the doctor. "Roseola is a very common and simple childhood virus. The other children may have been exposed like J.J., but by the time the rash develops, he is no longer contagious. The older children likely have immunity from having a lesser case earlier in their lives. It's common for the diagnosis to be confused at first with a severe infectious disease because of the high fever, and J.J. also has an ear infection that made his white blood cell count go up. That further confused us. The antibiotics have helped that, and they can be completed with oral medication now."

Benji asked the big question: "When can we go home?"

The doctor smiled. "You can all pack your bags and go as soon as I can sign J.J. out."

That was greeted with a big "Hurrah!" from the whole family.

As they were packing up to leave the hospital, Kelsey stopped to look at the ledge beneath the window. "What's this?" She turned around, holding a small blue egg. It was about half the size of a regular hen egg.

J.J. looked around as though he knew exactly what it was. "That's one of Bird's parrot eggs. That's where he sat while I was sick."

The family took the egg and the mystery and hurried out of the hospital.

CHAPTER THIRTY-FOUR

The weather continued to be unseasonably warm for November. The Bankers seemed happy for additional time out on the water or surf, before the chill of winter forced them inside. The northerners who had come to the area for duck hunting found they spent more time fishing and sunning than sitting in cold duck blinds.

At Sailor's Rest, Administrator Smith kept his radio on his desk, tuned to the NOAA weather band for updates on the weather from the tropics. Most recently, the tropical wave had become an official tropical storm on a gradual west-by-northwest track. Smith met with his "weather safety team" in the afternoon. "Well," he said, "we've been lucky so far this year, and I'm not saying this storm will affect us, but let's get prepared."

The team consisted of key personnel from the nursing facility, including James Triplett, as well as department heads and the business office personnel. Plans had long been in place and were revised periodically for storm preparation. They included preparing the facility to defend against and minimize damage from winds and flooding water. The plan also included a consideration for a possible evacuation of the facility. Each resident was considered in terms of any special needs for evacuation and whether the resident had any alternatives, such as the option of going to the mainland with family for a short period until the facility was judged safe after a storm. Arrangements had already been made for inland mainland facilities to accommodate residents and accept the staff to help care for the residents and maintain continuity of care. After considering the residents' care, the team moved on to plans for the temporary movement of the valuable art and antiques from Sailor's Rest. Smith concluded the meeting with the hope that none of these plans would need to be executed, but he noted, "Forewarned is forearmed."

Down in the Bum Boat Lounge, Charles Murphy was sitting in his usual chair, sipping a cup of coffee and nibbling on his morning sweet roll. After his recent conversation with Eddie, he had decided to move up his timetable for his Edith campaign.

As soon as Edith had concluded her "sitter-cize" class, she made her way to the lounge, knowing that her friend Murphy would be there. "Charles, are you feeling any better today? You know that I've been worried about you."

"Edith, my pet, I feel weaker every day. The doctor had some bad news for me. He says that what I have is worse than cancer. He doesn't know if I'll be here for Christmas or not."

"Isn't there anything that can be done?"

"There are treatments, but he doesn't think they will help. There is a new experimental medicine that is my best chance, but I can't do it."

"For heaven's sake, why not?"

"It's like everything else in life, Edith. It's the money. My insurance is just about played out, and even if there were enough money in my insurance account, they wouldn't pay because this treatment is considered experimental. Can you beat that? My only chance, and it turns out it's an untested experimental treatment."

Edith had no answer for that. She only sat there at his table, held his hand, and frowned. An occasional tear trickled down her cheek. She dabbed at the tears and tried to make some semblance of a smile, but it wouldn't come. "Why don't you let me help you with the payment?"

"Edith, you've helped me so much, too much. You really have. I couldn't accept any more of your help. Don't worry about me. I've led a good life. In fact, I've lived more than two or three lives in my years on earth. And I've lived a life full of adventures that would have killed less lucky men years ago. I'm okay—

really, I am—and if I don't beat this, my only regret is that I met you so late in my life." Then Murphy added, "But I did meet you."

"You must let me help. You find out how much that treatment costs and let me know." After a long, sincere hug and a smooch on the cheek that drew stares from other residents in the lounge, Edith went back to her suite.

Murphy continued to sit at his table with his topped-off cup of coffee, Danish, cards, and newspaper. The look on his face was that of a man without a care, one who had a firm grip on his place in the world, it was a look that in one word would be called *smug*.

CHAPTER THIRTY-FIVE

That evening in the Triplett house, there was a sense of thankfulness for J.J.'s recovery. Although his symptoms could have been a sign of severe illness, fortunately his virus had run a short—and according to the doctors, benign—course. He still had that lacey telltale rash that was a sign of the virus, but it was fading. He was on antibiotics for the ear infection that had only served to complicate his diagnosis. Otherwise, he was back to being his usual happy J.J.

James had one question. "J.J., tell me, who visited you in the hospital?"

"Mommy and you visited me. Those ladies in the funny clothes …"

"You mean the nurses?"

"Yeah, the nurses and the doctor and the nice ladies with the food visited me. Benji and Kelsey only came to take me home." J.J. stuck out his tongue to kid them for not visiting.

"Did anyone else visit you? What about Johnny and his bird?"

"Oh, they didn't visit. They stayed with me the whole time."

"And they talked to you?"

"Uh-huh. Well, Johnny talked, and Bird just whistled. He's a whistling bird and not the talking type."

"Did they come home with you?"

"They didn't come home in the car with us. That's silly. There wouldn't be room. But they are here. I saw Johnny up in the big oak tree when we got home. I think I saw Bird too. I know I heard Bird's whistle."

James's investigation of J.J.'s friends would not likely clear up the mystery of Johnny and the bird, so he decided to take another approach. "Does the bird lay eggs? We found a small egg in your hospital room."

"Well, it's not mine. I did not lay an egg!"

Everyone chuckled at J.J.'s statement, but Benji wouldn't look James in the eye. James picked up on this. "Benji, do you want to tell us something?"

Benji looked sheepish, and he looked at the ceiling as he answered. "I know this stripper who works at the hospital."

James took a moment to process this. Then it dawned on him what Benji meant. "You mean that you know a *striper*, a candy striper, a high school girl who volunteers at the hospital."

"Yeah, that. She's a candy stripper at the hospital."

"And?"

"And I heard that J.J. was seeing his imaginary friend and bird, so I asked Suzy to put an egg in the room. She thought it was a dumb idea, and I didn't think she would do it until we found it when packing up."

James was both amused and relieved. There was no punishment needed for this simple prank, and it was sort of funny. "Well, at least we've solved one mystery. Now we need to watch the weather."

James turned on the television, and the timing was perfect. As the screen lit up, the weatherperson was just beginning to give the long-term forecast. "We are continuing to track the tropical storm as it follows the west-by-northwest path from the west coast of Africa across the Atlantic." The weatherperson pointed to the east coast of the Carolinas and said, "We predict that this high-pressure system will cause the storm to steer a more northerly course and that this will turn out to be a fish storm, but as we know, hurricanes are, if anything, unpredictable. Follow along with us as we keep monitoring this storm."

As the announcer went on to more immediate local weather, Benji got out his hurricane tracker map and began plotting.

155

"Gosh, the last hurricane that followed this track slammed into Wilmington."

James looked at Benji's map and commented, "I remember that storm. There was so much damage that many homes were never rebuilt. Let's hope this really does stay out to sea, but we'll put aside some extra food and have some bottled water available, along with batteries. We'll keep the car gassed up so we can avoid lines at the pumps and evacuate quickly if we need to. Nan, a lot of this will be up to you since I'll be needed at the nursing home if the storm gets close."

Benji said, "I'll help too. If the storm gets that close, schools will be out."

CHAPTER THIRTY-SIX

The next morning found Captain Smith taking a moment of fresh air on a bench in front of Sailor's Rest. It was one of his favorite spots since it had such an excellent view of the bay. But today was a bit different. The air felt too muggy for this early in the morning. It usually felt fresh and cool at this time, but now it felt...tropical.

As he took a few minutes to enjoy the morning and contemplate the possible storm, Mildred Triplett Cromer came from the parking lot, ready for her morning. Smith wanted to pick her brain as a lifelong Banker. "Top of the morning to you, Mildred. Can I bend your ear a minute?"

"Sure, Captain Smith. What can I do for you?"

"This weather, it's kind of unusual."

"It's different all right, but I've seen it before."

"What do you think of that big storm?"

"I'd watch out. The weather's muggy, and my bunion hurts. As my pappy said, 'I think we're in for a blow.'"

"That's what I think, too. We'd better be prepared to enact our hurricane disaster plan."

....

Smith was not the only one making plans. Murphy had his own plan to execute. His first step was to be gone for the morning. He made arrangements for public transportation and got a ride to an

157

area on the mainland in Morehead City, close to the hospital and a complex of medical office buildings. He made arrangements for a return trip in the afternoon and hailed a cab to a nearby bar. Over a glass of his favorite libation, he killed some time that would be equivalent to the length of a medical visit.

His main errand was a visit to a local pawnshop–jewelry store to discuss antique coins. Behind the counter was a Murphy look-alike, his white hair pulled back into a ponytail. The main difference was a gaudy gold chain about the pawnbroker's neck. Murphy stepped up to the counter and addressed his look-alike. "I'd like your opinion on some oddities I have here."

The pawnbroker looked curious. "Okay, what do you have?"

"Here are a couple of items that were given to me as 'lucky stones.' Can you see anything special here?" Murphy laid the likely coins on the counter.

The broker took out his loupe, placed it over his left eye, and turned a stone over and over. "You know these are more than curious stones, or you wouldn't be here. They have the appearance of stones because they're encrusted in calcium. It looks as though they have been in the elements for years, perhaps hundreds of years." The broker took the two stones to a microscope and noticed a subtle difference between them. "This one is, underneath the accumulated crust, a Spanish piece of eight —silver. The other is slightly heavier. My gem scope picks up an amber sheen, even through the calcification. I'd say that that one is a Spanish doubloon, sometimes termed a *pistolé*. In the sixteenth and up to the mid-nineteenth century, these were the world currency. They were more credible and of more stable value than the dollar or pound sterling. The retail is likely five to seven hundred dollars per coin when cleaned up. The historical value is as much or more than the monetary. Cleaning these coins may actually diminish the retail value. Where did you say you found these? You haven't been poking around the *Queen Anne's Revenge* wreck site, have you?"

"I'm sorry, I'm not at liberty to say. But I may be able to obtain many more where I got these. Would you be able to handle that?"

"It may take a little time, but I can handle all you can haul in here."

"I'll be back." And with that, Murphy picked up his two stones and left the shop.

Back at the home, he was ready for Edith's afternoon visit.

Edith appeared as he had expected. "I see you're back from your morning excursion."

"I would have much preferred to be here, my love. Doctors give me the creeps."

"Can you share what the doctor said?"

"I've got what they call an immune problem. It's called an autoimmune disease. My body appears to think it's all an accidental splinter in my hand. It appears that my body is attacking itself. There are medications available, but there are no guarantees in life. He may be able to control it. The doctor continues to suggest that without the treatments, I may not see the New Year."

"Oh dear, you must have the treatments. I don't think I could bear parting with you, not so soon after losing my dear Albert."

"Unfortunately, my insurance still is balking at covering the treatment. My condition is rare, and though the treatment may save my life, it's not approved. My budget doesn't allow for any frivolous activities like lifesaving experimental treatments."

Edith sat very still for several moments. "Exactly how much are you going to need to get yourself well?"

"Edith, I hate to tell you. As generous as you are, it's too much."

"Perhaps you should let me be the judge of that. I'll decide whether I can afford to help my best friend or not."

"My initial treatment would cost thirty thousand dollars. Then follow-up treatments would likely be needed, or else there would be no use undergoing the initial … I think he called it an induction. Yes, he said the initial induction would cost thirty thousand dollars. He said most people end up mortgaging their home to pay for this treatment, but I don't even have a home. I never needed one; the sea was my home."

Edith was breathing rapidly. Murphy wasn't surprised that the price of his "treatments" had stunned her. She sat motionless for several minutes, and then in a hoarse voice she said, "Murphy, that's a lot of money. Amy and I had words regarding my little gifts for you. She doesn't understand our relationship. I want to help you. Let me think of the best way to do this. We need to be smart. I know that later on Amy will approve, but initially, she'll need some persuading." Edith gave Murphy a hug and a little kiss on the cheek in an almost secretive way. Then she retreated to her suite to figure how she could get Murphy such a large sum of money.

....

Eddie, the ever-present janitor with a big vacuum cleaner and bigger ears, was spending inordinate amounts of time in the hall outside Edith's suite. That afternoon, he heard a heated telephone conversation between Edith and someone he supposed was her daughter. He could hear bits and pieces of her daughter's side of the conversation too because Edith's receiver was adjusted for her poor hearing.

"Amy, you heard me right. That's thirty thousand dollars for needed medical treatments."

"… not over… I'll stop… your lawyer."

"I worked just as hard as Albert for what we've earned, and you're well taken care of. Now I can afford to help out Murphy without affecting my income, so I intend to do it."

"… no check… stop payment."

"Well, you do what you need to do, and I'll do what I must, so there." With that, Edith hung up. Eddie couldn't tell if Edith had hung up on her daughter or if they had mutually ended the conversation, but he knew that Murphy would want to know.

Back at Murphy's roost in the lounge, Eddie disclosed his findings. "Edith's taken the bait. I heard her on the phone. She's getting some push-back from her daughter, but she's a stubborn old woman. I'll bet that she'll get you the full amount one way or another."

Murphy only smiled.

....

It was time for the evening news and weather report in the Triplett household. Like everyone else on the island, they were paying close attention to the weather. When the weatherperson came on the screen, everyone gathered about the television to watch closely. Benji had his tracking chart and wax pencil out, ready to update his chart.

The broadcaster stood aside so the map could be easily viewed. "As you can see, the tropical storm has now achieved sustained winds of seventy-five miles per hour. This storm now officially qualifies as a category 1 hurricane and has been officially named Emily. The course is not showing much of a change at present. There is still a chance that it could take a northern turn and miss the Carolinas' coast, but we need to start our just-in-case preparations. It looks like it could make landfall in about three or four days. Please keep tuned in to get the latest forecast."

James looked at his family and said that they needed to start getting ready. They called friends on higher ground on the mainland and were told they would be welcome to visit to wait out the storm. Nan would be sure the car was serviced, and they would be ready to leave when the notice was given.

CHAPTER THIRTY-SEVEN

The next afternoon, Edith met Murphy in the lounge. "Murphy, I hope you're feeling better today."

"Edith, the doctor's visit yesterday tired me out too much. I'm so weak I can barely sit up. But that's enough about me. How are you today?"

"I'm okay, but I had an argument with my daughter. She doesn't want me to write your check."

"I can understand that, and I really didn't expect you to help out old Murph."

"But I can still do a bank transfer. I have a niece at the bank who will still allow me to do that. I called her this morning. I will need your account information to make the transfer. Is that a problem?"

Murphy thought about this for a few minutes. Edith was as gullible as any of his previous female marks. He saw no malice in the sweet old lady. "I'll get the information after supper this evening. I really appreciate this. I'll be forever grateful."

He conferred with Eddie later in the afternoon. Eddie had a definite opinion. "Man, you've sold her big time. She's eating out of your hand. Give her your numbers, and go get your money outta the bank."

. . . .

Benji persuaded Kelsey to help with the excavation of the hole under the big live oak tree. As Benji turned over spades of sandy dirt, Kelsey examined the dirt for the shell-like stones that Mr. Murphy had found so interesting. She heard a flapping noise in the higher branches of the tree and saw the scarlet, green, and yellow colors of Johnny's bird. And as she expected, she could make out the shadow of a boy who must have been her age. At least she thought she saw Johnny, but because of his faded, worn clothes and his dark skin color, he blended in with the shadows and foliage of the trees. She asked Benji, "Do you see him? Do you see Johnny and his bird?"

Benji stopped his digging long enough to look up into the aged tree. He didn't want to admit that he had heard what might have been wings flapping, but he couldn't see anything through the sweat in his eyes and the glare created by the afternoon sun. "I seem to hear something in the tree, but I can't see a thing. Anyway, look how many stones we've collected. There are probably a hundred stones here, and they're all about the same size. I don't know if they are worth anything, but Mr. Murphy was awfully interested in my lucky stone, so I want more of them. And just look—the deeper I dig, the more stones I find."

Kelsey had filled up three burlap sacks with stones. They were so heavy that she couldn't move them, and Benji had to drag them up the hill to the house. He said, "Just think, Kelsey— if these were clams instead of stones, they would be worth… well, they may be worth as much as fifty dollars."

....

Nan was busy in the house. With the possibility of a big blow, she was preparing for the decision to either weather the storm or leave if an evacuation order was issued for the island. Bankers had most of this work bred into them as children. Candles, lanterns, batteries, and jugs of water were stocked, stored, and rechecked regularly for freshness. Canned and nonperishable food was put up so that the family could weather a long power outage. The cars were gassed and ready for a prolonged drive or, more likely, a prolonged wait in line to exit the island. Local

163

relatives had advised Nan and James of these needed preparations, and the pair had listened, so there was not too much panic in preparing for their first big storm—just a little.

Nan was rechecking the cupboard for the tenth or perhaps one hundredth time when she heard a knock on the door. It was Ms. Groner, Kelsey's teacher. Nan actually welcomed the interruption, since she knew she was doing repetitive tasks mainly to quiet her nerves. "Ms. Groner, what a surprise. Aren't you preparing for the storm?"

"Lawd, honey, I stay ready. No storm's gonna find me unprepared. Can I help you with anything? I know y'all are sort of new to this, and it can be frenetic, but we think of it as the price of living in such a beautiful place."

"I think we're all set. We're keeping an ear to the radio to see if Emily will make that northern turn or be on our front doorstep. We've planned for both."

"That sounds like the plan of a lifelong Banker. One reason I came by today was to talk about Kelsey."

Nan had suspected there might be another reason for the sudden appearance of Ms. Groner. They had become acquainted with her, but she was not one of their close friends. "Is something going on with Kelsey that we should know about?"

"Kelsey's a model student. She's smart, polite, motivated, and always willing to help in class. She's almost a little teacher— always willing to help me with the student who needs extra attention. But she has been telling some peculiar stories about things going on in… well, around your house."

"I suspect she has told you about Johnny and the bird."

"Yes, she mentioned J.J.'s friend, and since his trip to the hospital, the stories have become more detailed."

"She does have an active imagination, and we've tried to downplay J.J.'s imaginary friend, but you know how kids love to exaggerate."

Ms. Groner offered a knowing and sympathetic smile but had something else on her mind. "A lot of people living on the Banks have had experiences with unexplained phenomena. It may come from the generations of isolation, or perhaps it's living close to nature with all the eerie sounds and effects from the island weather and wildlife. But stories abound of spirits or haunts. You may call them ghosts and goblins and tell stories about them at Halloween. I can assure you that we do all that on the island, but we also have more than our share of legends, myths, and unexplainable events. Kelsey's Johnny sounds like he may be more than an imaginary friend."

Nan felt like the conversation with Ms. Groner was evolving into an *X-Files* episode. She was beginning to feel a bit uncomfortable. "Uh, okay, where is all this going?"

"I can see that I've startled you a bit, but it was not my intention to frighten you or to make you feel uncomfortable. Now I'm not some hysterical female, and I'm usually so normal that I'm almost bland. But J.J.'s experiences are very familiar to me. They are so familiar that I feel compelled to share them with you. It's just that I have had some experience with these events and thought I could give you some advice. As a child on the island, I saw some things that could not be explained. It was nothing sinister, and my family played along with my imaginary friend. My friend was a little blue-eyed girl with blond curls. She wore clothing that was totally unlike anything I had ever seen. She was barefoot and carried a cloth doll. She would speak to me, but not to anyone else. She told me her name was Virginia."

"You think that she was…"

"Yes, exactly, I think I was speaking to the spirit of Virginia Dare. Since then, I've looked in books. The girl's clothing was appropriate to that period, though at four years old, I didn't know anything about the Lost Colony or Elizabethan customs. So how could I have imagined such a detailed picture of Virginia? Since then, I've heard of other similar cases of apparitions, or you may call them hauntings. But 'hauntings' implies an ominous presence. An apparition—the word I prefer—is benign, or more likely helpful. I think that J.J.'s friend Johnny and his bird are more than imaginary friends. I suspect that J.J. has achieved a connection to a spirit. This Johnny may be a spirit that has lain dormant for centuries with no concept of time. After all, after we leave this mortal coil, what is the importance of time? J.J. may have awakened this spirit and achieved a connection. And that spirit's connection to J.J. may be why he was able to accompany him to the hospital.

"I know you're busy, but when I heard Kelsey's story, it brought back vivid memories from my childhood, and I wanted to share my story with you before we got too carried away with all these storm activities."

Nan asked, "Do you still see Virginia?"

"I haven't seen her since I was about Kelsey's age," said Ms. Groner, "but there are times when I feel a strong presence."

"Doesn't it frighten you?"

"No, I don't feel her often, but when I do, it's not scary; it's a comfort. I don't consider myself haunted or possessed. I think I've received a gift of a companion—a presence that is there when I need her. I think that I carry a bit of Virginia with me all the time. She comes to me when I need her, wherever I am. I feel blessed to have a bit of her with me."

After Ms. Groner's visit, Nan had mixed feelings. First, she wondered if it was safe for Kelsey to continue in a classroom with this strange person. Then she decided that this encounter fit with the ambience of the island, and the teacher was sharing her best advice. At least she was harmless.

166

CHAPTER THIRTY-EIGHT

In the administrator's office at Sailor's Rest, the NOAA radio crackled with the alarm sound that indicated an urgent weather bulletin was imminent.

"Hurricane Emily has now achieved the status of a high category 2 hurricane. The course continues to be west-by-northwest, and a northern turn is expected, but the population of the Carolinas and Virginia coast should continue storm preparations that may include evacuation. No evacuation order has been issued yet, but please stay tuned to the NOAA frequencies."

Administrator Smith had experienced alerts many times. He had a plan for handling weather events and called his facilities manager, James Triplett. James took the call and made notes. They had thoroughly discussed the emergency plan daily, so James's duty now was to implement the plan, hoping for the best but preparing for the worst. Like at home, all loose outside objects were secured. Also, in the facility, generators were double-checked, foodstuffs and supplies had been double-ordered and received. The irreplaceable art and antique furniture were removed to a mainland warehouse. James continued down his checklist to ensure that the facility was as secure as possible.

While James was checking his list, the human resources director was doing the same with hers. Mildred was calling all the staff to be sure that all staffing was filled and that all employees would be able to get to work for their shifts. She was also making plans for the possible evacuation, to be sure that those sites accepting Sailor's Rest residents would be able to handle added Sailor's Rest staff as well. The staff was prepared to work in the accepting sites if needed.

On the resident-care side, the director of care was notifying families and making preparations for the storm. Some families would be able to take their family members home for the duration of the storm, and the residents needed their medications and treatment plans to go home with them. Others would stay or be evacuated with the facility's evacuation plan if it came to that point. Arrangements were made to send meds and treatments and even to send one-on-one chaperones with residents if needed. Volunteer, regular EMS, and even public-school buses could be enlisted for additional help.

....

After lunch, Murphy was in the lounge, occupying his usual chair. He had his pack of cards and cribbage board on the table.

Soon Edith approached his table with her slow, tottering walk. She sat down across the table from him. "Do you think we'll be evacuated?"

"Oh, no one knows what a hurricane will do. Not even the great Neptune could predict its path." He snickered almost to himself and said, "Maybe that's why they call them hurricanes. They're no more predictable than most females."

"Well, I don't want to leave, but Amy says safety first. By the way, I talked to my niece. She said that she would help me with the money transfer. Can you give me those numbers?"

Murphy handed over a folded sheet of paper that contained his bank account number. Edith leaned over and kissed him lightly on the cheek and left the lounge to call her niece. Murphy noticed that as she made her way back to her suite, she had the hint of some spring in her step. He could not help but think, *Well, I guess that is a thirty-thousand-dollar improvement in her gait. I hope she will think it was worth it.*

Back at the Triplett home, J.J. was playing down by the sound. Benji and Kelsey had not returned from school. Nan had taken a break from storm preparations to watch her youngest son. J.J. was jabbering along, talking to his friend whom she had yet to see or hear. J.J. said, "My mama and my dad be at home tonight. Dad say a hurricane's comin'."

Nan thought she had heard wrong. "J.J., who are you talking to? And why are you talking like that?"

"I'm talking to Johnny, and that's just how he talks. He says everyone talks like that. Johnny says a big storm is coming. He remembers a bad storm, and this one will be worse."

Nan didn't see anyone, but this had been going on long enough that she really didn't expect to. Soon an egret standing on a piling grabbed J.J.'s attention. He began to play at the water's edge. As J.J. played, he whistled a tune. Nan had heard him demonstrate his newly learned whistling ability, but she hadn't realized he had become proficient in whistling tunes. She recognized the tune he was whistling. It wasn't perfect, but she could make out a song she hadn't heard since childhood. It was "Old Dan Tucker."

CHAPTER THIRTY-NINE

By six o'clock in the evening, the NOAA radio at Sailor's Rest was again buzzing.

"Hurricane Emily continues on a generally westward course. It passed over the island nation of Bermuda with 100-mile-per-hour winds and decimated the island. The storm is predicted to take a northward turn in the next twelve hours. Warnings are being anticipated for the Carolinas in the next twelve hours."

....

Edith visited Murphy in his room. She rarely saw him there, as a proper lady addressed a gentleman friend only in public areas rather than private, but on this occasion, she felt that some privacy was needed. "Charlie, I've done it. My niece helped with the transfer, and it's done. I hope that this will be enough to help your medical condition, and I hope that it won't change our relationship."

Murphy was touched by the care and sacrifice of his octogenarian friend. "Edith, that is so much more than I could have expected. I pray that your selfless gift will restore the health of this old salt." He had tears in his eyes as he gently held her hands and leaned forward to kiss her cheek.

Her cheeks darkened with a slight blush as she received the kiss. She seemed embarrassed by his unusual show of emotion and sought to make an excuse to leave him alone. "I must get back to my room, and you need your rest." She carefully rose from the chair with all the care demanded by the bones of an elderly lady and left his room.

Murphy prepared for bed. There was some concern among the staff that with all the uncertainty of the storm, the residents would be too upset to get their needed rest. Murphy slept very well.

························

The Tripletts were also anxious about the coming storm. Nan had the family's SUV ready to go. Bags were packed; groceries were loaded. Everything that could be stuffed in the vehicle in advance was included. Other items had been boxed and placed in the kitchen where they could be placed in the old Suburban in minutes. Nan didn't realize that in the third-row footwell, three sacks of the peculiar rocks Andy had unearthed from beneath the big oak tree had found a home.

CHAPTER FORTY

The following morning, the winds came out of the east. There was a muggy, tropical feel to the air. Lifelong residents of the Banks had worried looks as they gazed at the horizon. These experienced Bankers didn't need a NOAA report to know that severe weather was approaching.

But the official NOAA alert was coming into line with their lifetime of intuition. "Upper-level steering currents have not generated as much energy as anticipated. The current course of the storm is expected to veer only marginally from its current west-northwest path. The winds continue to increase in velocity, and the storm may be a category 4 by the time it makes landfall late tomorrow afternoon. Evacuation orders will be expected today."

In the Triplett household, the excitement over their first hurricane as new Bankers was building. Everything that could be considered a loose item had already been moved inside or nailed down. Storm shutters were closed. The list of final preparations included cutting off the electricity and water. Kelsey and J.J. were getting their favorite comfort stuffed animals together. School was out due to the storm, and Nan was preparing to leave before the official evacuation order.

James had a special duty for Benji. At fourteen, he was more than capable of assisting residents and moving their belongings. James had volunteered his son's services to assist in the evacuation. After a quick breakfast, James gave Nan and the younger kids a quick hug, and in two separate vehicles, they pulled out of their driveway together.

Nan followed James's truck till it turned to the right to the nursing home. Nan and the two smaller children headed straight for the causeway and bridge. The family planned to meet at the Friendly Market in Morehead City later in the day.

....

At Sailor's Rest, Murphy was anticipating the evacuation, but he also had more personal plans. Captain Smith had called all personnel to assist in an orderly evacuation, but Murphy had asked him for Eddie's services as a driver for an important doctor's appointment. Smith was unaware of any severe change in Murphy's health, but Murphy had always been secretive. He supposed that even with the increased activity in the facility that he could do without Eddie's services for a couple of hours.

Though traffic was beginning to pick up, Eddie and Murphy were able to make adequate progress into Morehead City. The physician's appointment time Murphy had designated was not relevant. It was fictitious.

Today was Murphy's day to cash out. His first stop was his bank. The bank manager knew Murphy. Over his years at Sailor's Rest, he had made several sizable deposits and had amassed an account of over three hundred thousand dollars. Now was the time to complete his scheme and leave eastern North Carolina forever.

The local manager was working in a teller's cage since he was shorthanded. Several call-ins had occurred because of the upcoming evacuation. He was going to close the bank very soon anyway. "Well, Mr. Murphy, what can we do for you today?"

"Mr. Phelps, I've been a customer here for several years and increased my account on a regular basis."

"Yes, Mr. Murphy, we appreciate your patronage. You're a good customer."

"I appreciate that, but all good things must come to an end, and today I'm closing my account. I'll take it in one-hundred-dollar bills."

Phelps was taken aback. "I hope we have that much cash on hand. With the coming storm, things have been, well, irregular. Let me check the totals, and I'll get this done immediately. I hope we haven't done anything to offend you to make you take your business to another institution."

"No, no, I'm just feeling the urge to move on."

Phelps went into his office to calculate the amount of cash in Murphy's account. After several minutes, he returned to the teller's cage with a business envelope. "Here you are, Mr. Murphy. Now don't hang around too long in the coming storm. I hear it's going to be a record breaker."

Murphy looked at the envelope he had just been handed. He had expected to be given a bank bag for the funds, and the envelope looked much too thin for his account balance. He looked in the envelope and counted six one-hundred-dollar bills and twenty-nine cents. He felt his knees go weak. He broke out in a sweat. He felt his blood pressure rise so fast that he was concerned his head would literally explode. He addressed Phelps in a roaring voice, as though he actually was yelling into a hurricane. "Just what is the meaning of this, Phelps? I've got well over three hundred thousand in this rinky-dink bank! Now where is it?"

"Mr. Murphy, the bulk of your account was removed in the form of a bank transfer yesterday. Wasn't it done at your request? All the numbers were correct."

"It most certainly was not done at my request!" Then he thought a moment. Somewhere in his head a synapse fired, and he thought of his dear friend and favorite mark, Edith. He should have been mad, and he was indeed incensed, but at the same time, he couldn't keep from smiling. Slowly, like the gathering storm, the smile became a giggle and then finally an uproarious guffaw that could be heard across the floor of the bank.

Phelps was concerned for Murphy's health. "Can I get you anything? Perhaps you could use a glass of water. Or would you like to lie down in my office for a minute?"

"No, Phelps, thank you, but I'll be fine. The transfer merely slipped my mind for a moment. You know, I'm not getting any younger." With that, he wished Phelps a safe afternoon and exited the bank.

Eddie was waiting outside, and by the look on Murphy's face, he knew that things hadn't gone well in the bank.

Rather than having Eddie drive him, Murphy walked half a block to the pawnshop. The bells on the door jangled as he passed through the front door. The Murphy look-alike broker was behind the counter and did not seem too busy, considering the upcoming storm.

He smiled a knowing smile as he recognized Murphy. "Well, if it isn't the man with the Spanish gold and silver! Come on in. As you can see, everyone wants to get out of town, and they don't mind leaving their pawned goods till they get back. Do you have some more Spanish trinkets? I seem to recall that I priced those at five hundred per piece. That might have been a bit light. I've done some checking, and it's likely that I could go a bit higher per unit. I'll take them all day. And there is something else. Do you remember all that calcium that made it appear more like a stone than a coin?"

"Yep."

"Well, that's exactly what collectors want. They want as much of it encrusted as possible. It adds to the authenticity and the story. It actually adds to the value."

"I'm fairly certain I can get you more of those, perhaps many more. But I'm here for something else today."

"Okay, what have you brought me?"

Murphy opened up a brown paper bag and pulled out a velvet box with a crown in the center. "I have here a valuable Rolex watch. It's a real collector's item. I'll bet that you'll be able to sell it in no time flat."

"Ah, very impressive, Mr. Murphy. Down here we don't get very many Rolex specimens, and with the tech guys discovering beach property, there is plenty of disposable income."

The broker actually put on his white gloves and took the box as though it were a priceless diamond. He opened the box and broke out in a wide grin. "How much did you say you wanted for this watch?"

"I think that five thousand is a good number. The diamonds alone are worth that much."

"And how much did you pay for this watch?"

"I didn't actually pay for the watch. It was a gift."

"You're fortunate that you didn't pay for this. I'm afraid that your benefactor is the victim of a prank. The box undoubtedly housed a genuine Rolex watch at some point. But the watch inside is a cheap knock-off. It's similar to the kind you find sold by a street vendor in Times Square. There is no value here. I think that whoever gave you this watch was sold a bill of goods."

Murphy took his fake Rolex back and shoved it back in the brown bag. As he was turning around to walk out of the shop, he had one last comment for the broker. "She was a good salesman, a *very* good salesman." He shoved the brown bag in a trash bin on his way back down the street to find Eddie.

On the drive back to Sailor's Rest, very few words were traded between Eddie and Murphy. Murphy was disheartened that he had been played. He wanted to confront Edith to see if there was some logical reason for the bank and the watch, but down deep he knew. He had to appreciate being beaten at his own game.

CHAPTER FORTY-ONE

Murphy's ride back to Sailor's Rest was faster than his trip to Morehead City. The wind had begun to pick up, and the rain was becoming serious. Eddie's truck was buffeted by the wind coming from the east. The lanes to the mainland were bumper-to-bumper, but the lanes leading to the island were empty. As they reached the mainland side of the bridge leading to the island, the flashing blue lights of a local deputy met them. He warned them that in a few minutes the lanes onto the island would be closed so that all four lanes could be used to get off the island.

Back at the retirement home, people were on the move. The staff was assisting in moving residents into vans and buses. Murphy saw both James and young Benjamin helping get the residents and their needed possessions ready to travel.

Murphy went to his room to pack his few belongings and found a white envelope pinned to his pillow.

Murphy,

Thank you for a very entertaining stay at Sailor's Rest. You are very charming, and I can see how my sister, Emily, was taken with your rough good looks and stories of adventures on the high seas. You do remember Emily, don't you? She contributed a large amount to your bank account to help your multiple chronic ailments. You'll be happy to know that she is comfortable in her new home. Fortunately, she is not impoverished, and her retirement account will be restored in full by yesterday's contribution.

Friendship to you,
Edith

Murphy sat on the side of the bed. He remembered Emily. She was a sweet lady who, like all his conquests, had recently lost her husband and felt lonely. But more than lonely, she had felt like a fifth wheel to her family and lost in her big old house without her mate of a lifetime. Murphy had supplied a quality that her life had been lacking, and she had responded to his nurturing. Boy, had she responded.

Edith was different. Edith had seemed so innocent, but "seemed" was all it was. She had been as much a character in a play as Murphy had been. Perhaps he could speak to Edith. He got himself up off the bed, though now his legs seemed weak, and for the first time in years, he had to admit that he felt his age. The short walk to her suite in the most posh section of Sailor's Rest took far longer than usual. As he turned the corner into her wing, he saw the commotion of the evacuation. In a few steps, he reached Edith's suite. The door was standing wide open, which he thought was unusual. The room was bare. It was not bare in the sense that she had just been evacuated to the mainland for the storm. It was totally bare. Bureau drawers were empty; the closet was even lacking hangers. He turned to see one of the housekeepers.

"Oh, Mr. Murphy, your friend done left. Her daughter, Amy, done come and got her early this morning. She said she was taking her mama home to live with her a while. It was just too isolated here. She called it Hicksville. Now ain't that somethin'?"

Murphy turned around and headed back to his room. On the way, he ran into Eddie. Eddie had no more than gotten through the front door when Captain Smith had given him work handling the movement of records and medications for the residents being sent to other facilities.

Murphy said, "Never mind what Smith wants. We've got to

find young Benjamin. I saw him here when we got back from town."

"Yeah, he's handling luggage for the evacuation, but it's almost complete. We'd better get a move on, or we'll have to face that storm here without any support. They're even cutting off the power and water to the building till the storm passes."

"Don't worry about that. We've still got an opportunity to get a quick payday over at the Tripletts' house."

"I don't know exactly where they live."

"That's okay. Young Benjamin will show us. Find Master Triplett and see if old Dad will let you drive him to the evacuation site."

Benji wasn't difficult to find. He was loading one of the last hand trucks of suitcases into a bus. His dad was there as well.

Eddie approached the crowd gathered about the school bus that had been put into service to transport the residents. "James, this weather is beginning to get more severe. I'm leaving with Mr. Murphy right now. I'd be happy to take Benji with me. It may be another hour or two before everyone gets out of here. It would be safer to get Benji to the mainland as soon as possible."

James looked over at Benji. "What do you say? Do you want to get a head start over to Morehead now? You can go ahead and meet Mom, Kelsey and J.J. at the Friendly Produce Market. I'll be along soon."

The weather was getting more uncomfortable by the minute. Benji wanted to help his dad, but getting off the island seemed like a real good idea. "Okay, when will they leave?"

"We're ready right now," said Eddie. "We'll leave him at the Friendly Produce on Bridges Street, and you can meet them there as soon as you can."

"That sounds like a plan, Eddie. Thanks."

As the pickup left to go down the drive from the facility, James took a moment to look up at the truck. He saw Benji looking back through the rear window. For a moment, James had a chill and a sudden feeling that his eldest son was going into a terrible storm and that this might be the last sight of his boy.

CHAPTER FORTY-TWO

The aged pickup followed the winding lane from the facility to the highway. A turn to the right led to the bridge and the evacuation route. But the truck turned to the left, following a line of residences. The narrow island had one row of scattered residences to the left, with the beach and ocean beyond. On the right, there was a slight elevation and a row of more modest houses abutting the sound. Rain was already sideways from the beach side. The winds were coming in gusts so strong that Eddie had problems keeping the truck in a straight line. Garbage cans, deck chairs, and other pieces of debris flew across the highway. Several items bounced off the vehicle. With the surf already passing well under the beachfront houses, the highway was under water at several places, Hurricane landfall was not predicted for hours, but travel was already hazardous on the ocean road.

Benji knew when the truck turned left instead of right that he and his dad had been deceived. Sitting close between the two larger men, he felt bullied. "Mr. Murphy, why did we turn away from the bridge?"

"Benjamin, we need to take a little detour before we evacuate. Don't worry. We'll get you safe and sound to your family. We just don't see any reason to sit for an hour or two in line to cross the bridge when we have a short errand to do before."

Benji's concern had now turned to fright. He tried to voice his objection, but instead of the forceful voice he tried to emit, the whiny, cracking, adolescent voice that he detested came out.

"Please turn around right now, and let's go back to where it's safe. This storm is getting worse by the minute. I want to go back."

Murphy responded with a practiced, calm voice. "Benjamin, there's real treasure under your nose, and it's up to us who recognize it to reap that treasure. Didn't I tell you that that's the Banker way?"

"My rocks?"

"Yes, my boy, your rocks, your stones, or as I should say more correctly, our valuable Spanish pieces of eight and doubloons. Those lucky stones you showed me turned out to be Spanish coins, valuable Spanish coins. And I'm betting that piece of rotted wood and rusted iron was at one time a hasp of a treasure chest. From the size of the hasp and the bulk of the iron, it had to be a massive chest meant to hold something valuable. I think it was a chest the size of a freezer locker. I'm betting it's full of gold and silver coins that originated in a Spanish treasure ship and somehow ended up here on the island. With a little bit of your help, we can fill the back of this truck with those coins. They are worth more in the hands of collectors than the value of the gold. We can have a fortune."

As Murphy spoke, he had the lust for pirate's treasure in his eye. Benji had read in his pirate stories about how men could be driven insane by the lure of treasure. He knew that any further complaint from him would be useless.

Just then, a tree branch banged against the driver's side window hard enough to fracture the safety glass.

Eddie asked, "Where exactly is your house?"

Benji was too frightened by the storm and his companions to lie. "It's right here on the right." He pointed to a driveway two lots down.

The street was now completely covered with water. In the distance there was an explosion. Eddie observed, "That's a transformer. They go out in every big storm." The rare streetlights had been on in spite of it being early afternoon, but now they all blinked out. By the time the truck turned to the right and up the slight incline to the Triplett house, water was surging halfway up the drive to the pilings supporting the old house. Eddie parked the truck beneath the house, and the three made their way down the path to the ancient live oak tree.

Eddie looked in the tool locker beneath the house and retrieved a shovel, a clam rake, and a bushel basket previously used for the day's catch. The irony of the moment was not lost on Eddie. He hoped that they would have better luck today than other fishermen who had used the equipment before.

The small rise on which the house sat provided some break from the wind and torrential rain. Although the path was soaked and slippery, it was better than the street side of the house that faced the ocean. They reached the site where the earth had been disturbed by Benji's digging and found a crater full of water. Eddie went back to the house to retrieve a bucket to bail the water from the hole.

Benji wanted to leave. He wanted to run away, and he thought he could get away from Eddie and Mr. Murphy, but where could he go?

The waves from the ocean began to lap over the crest of the island. Every third or fourth wave would reach over the crest of the narrow island and stream down the opposite side, down the hill, and flow into the sound. Eddie's attempts at bailing were futile. Water was flowing in faster than he could bail. The howl of the wind was so severe that even though Mr. Murphy was yelling at the top of his voice, but all that could be heard was the wind.

Then, as though a light had been switched off, the wind died. The waves receded, and though there was massive flooding on the ocean side of the crest, it was no longer breeching the island. The clouds had been so low that Benji felt he could reach up and touch them, but now he could see some clearing of the sky above. He was even able to see the late-afternoon sun.

Eddie began to clear the water from Benji's hole with better effect. Suddenly, he called to Murphy. "Well, lookee, lookee here."

. . . .

James arrived at the Friendly Produce expecting to see Nan, Kelsey, J.J., and Benji.

Nan looked up in relief as his truck turned into the gravel parking lot, but she instantly knew something was wrong when she saw that Benji was not in the truck. "Where's Benji?" were her only words. She didn't need any others. It was simultaneously a scream of panic and an indictment that James had allowed her oldest son to be lost somewhere in a hurricane.

James couldn't believe that Benji had not arrived; he should have been there over an hour ago. Nan had seen no sign of Benji or his two companions. James jumped back in the truck and headed back to the bridge. He turned onto the exit to the approach the bridge and found the bridge blocked off with saw horses and patrol cars with flashing blue lights. He approached a deputy who was having problems keeping upright in the wind in spite of his ample foul-weather gear.

James said, "Move that barricade. I've got to find my son."

"Sorry, sir. The bridge isn't safe. We've already had cars pushed sideways by the wind. We almost lost one off the side of the bridge."

"You haven't seen a rusty Jeep pickup come through?"

"You mean Eddie? I saw him going onto the island earlier. He had an old dude in his truck. But I haven't seen him return. I figured he was in one of the vans evacuating the nursing home."

"Look, I've got to find my son, and I'm afraid he's still on the island."

"Sheriff says the evacuation is complete, and there's no one left on the island. It's getting pretty beat up. If he's there, I hope he's found some cover in a high place. I'm sorry, but I just can't let you go over to the island. The sheriff won't allow it."

James lamented, "I don't know what I'll tell my wife. She allowed Benji to help me with the evacuation of Sailor's Rest on the condition that I'd take care of him. And now I've let her down." As James said this, he began to cry. He was afraid he had lost his son.

CHAPTER FORTY-THREE

Eddie bent over and picked a round, calcified stone from the pit. The massive amount of wave water cresting the top of the ridge had worked like a sluice to wash away the sand and debris, leaving the heavier calcium-encrusted coins.

Murphy bellowed a joyful order to both Eddie and Benji. "Hurry, fill up that basket! Eddie, dump it in the truck and get back here. Benjamin, start piling up the coins. You can keep Eddie busy taking the basket to the truck."

Soon Eddie had made several trips to the truck and reported the bed was half full. The wind from the west began to freshen. The sky above was still clear and as blue as possible, but an ominous bank of clouds as high as Benji could see was obscuring the mainland.

. . . .

Experiencing the calm period of the eye, James got in his truck, planning to drive through the barricade if the deputy wasn't going to move it.

The deputy reached his arm in through the open window and put his fleshy hands on James's steering wheel. "James, we'll search high and low for Benji. Really, we will. But you can't go back till the storm passes, and we've still got the backside to go through. You know that."

James did know that. Pangs of guilt and remorse flooded through him. As of now, he was totally helpless to do anything to help his son. He felt dejected and defeated, and worst of all, he had to tell Nan that he had no idea where or how Benji was.

....

When the rain resumed, it began as a sprinkle. The wind was initially warm, almost balmy. That lasted only minutes. Soon the wind picked up from the west. Leaves on the trees began to rustle, and dead leaves from the ground were stripped from their position and violently hurled like spears at the three figures on the bank. By now the bed of the pickup was over half full of coins, but there was no place to take shelter. Soon shingles began to peel from the roof of the Triplett house. Strong gusts became frequent, and the exposed wooden surface of the roof was pried open by the tremendous wind. By now, the pier where Benji had spent so many days fishing in the sound was totally covered by the water that had been driven from the rivers into the sound and now was challenging the banks of the island.

The three figures were holding onto the low branches of the big oak tree; otherwise, they would be blown away. The frame of the house began to break away. Benji could see the bed he had slept in last night being stripped of sheets before the mattress and box spring took to the air like kites. He last saw his bed's box spring as it bounced down the driveway. It reminded him of a pogo stick as it hit the driveway on its edge and bounced high in the air before hitting again and rolling away end over end, finally disappearing from sight.

Benji was entranced by the destruction of his family's home, but he did chance a look toward the sound and was even more horrified to see that the water had risen well over the pier and was coming further up the bank with each surging wave. At this pace the water would soon be at the base of the old oak tree.

Above the roar of the wind, he heard the crunch of metal. The old Jeep pickup was being pushed backward by the wind. When the back corner hung momentarily on a piling that was supporting the remnants of the Triplett house, the truck veered sideways. Murphy saw his fortune slipping away and yelled, "No, no, not now!" The wind was howling so fiercely that Benji had to read his lips.

Murphy wanted the treasure more than he wanted his life. He released his grasp on the old oak and literally flew after the Jeep. At that moment the wind caught under the truck and flipped it on its top. Murphy had been carried up the hill as though in flight. One foot pivoted on the door of the Jeep as it began its flip upside down. He almost seemed acrobatic as he bounded on the overturning truck, and then he was airborne and out of sight. The bed of the truck now sat wedged into a dune that the Tripletts had hoped would serve as a windbreak for their home.

The water had reached the base of the tree. Benji managed to hang on to a branch and pull himself out of the water. Eddie decided to scramble to higher ground. The remaining pilings of the house were several feet higher, but it was uncertain whether that height would make a difference. He let go of the oak and was blown up the hill to the skeleton of the wrecked house. As he passed one of the remaining pilings, he attempted to catch it. For a moment he grasped the piling, but his fingers couldn't hold. He skated across the concrete slab foundation, past his wrecked Jeep, and was dragged down toward the ocean. Now Benji was alone. As much as Murphy and Eddie had frightened him, being alone in the storm was worse.

CHAPTER FORTY-FOUR

The rest of the Triplett family had planned to stay with relatives in the Raleigh area, but they would not go far till they had found Benji. An evacuation center had been opened in the local Presbyterian Church, and they settled down on cots to pray and wait. Nan overcame her initial angst, and she huddled with her family, holding James, Kelsey, and J.J. closely as the storm raged and the old building creaked and rattled.

....

Benji climbed up the ancient oak on the side opposite the wind. Now the frothy waves were over the bottom branches of the tree and almost covering the concrete base of the ruin of the Triplett home. By the time he mounted a higher branch, he could no longer see any sign of the house. It was covered with water. The tops of the island's scrubby trees were all that was left of the island until or if the storm passed.

Benji climbed even higher up the tree. Now he was on the highest branch he could reach, and yet the water was almost up to his waist. The bark was slippery against his fingers, and the thin trunk was swaying violently and seemed close to splitting with each gust.

Benji thought that he could never be more scared than he was right then, and then he heard the thunder. It was so loud that for a moment it drowned out the roar of the wind. He was going to count as his father had taught him, to gauge how far away the lightning was, but before he could count, the flash occurred. It was so bright that he almost lost his grip on the thin branch he clutched like a lifeline.

Then he heard a flapping sound—like wings. He knew his ears were playing tricks on him, but he also heard a faint voice. "Hold onto me," the voice whispered.

Benji looked up and saw the little black boy in rags. He appeared to be thinner but taller than Kelsey, almost the same size. Benji had never seen Johnny. He had believed that Johnny and his bird were imaginary. He still was not certain. Johnny might be imaginary, but more importantly, he was here.

Benji reached a hand up to Johnny. Johnny grabbed his hand and pulled. The pull was just enough to make a difference, helping Benji go up another branch. The bird was there and didn't seem to be phased by the howling wind and driving rain.

Benji heard the voice again. It was the gentle voice of a child. "Don't you be scairt. Johnny's not scairt. Bird's not scairt, so don't you be afraid."

Benji looked up at the boy. "Johnny, will you stay with me?"

"Me and Bird will stay here. We're here always, but you got to climb higher."

"I can't climb higher."

"You can. I know you can. Now hold my hand and climb."

Not only was Johnny higher, but he had somehow moved to another fork of the tree. Benji had to totally release his grasp on the limbs of one fork to reach the limbs of the next one. He released his grip and found Johnny's hand. It was the hand of a spirit that he had denied existed till a minute ago.

As he did so, he smelled the aroma of ozone in the air, and his foot began to tingle. Then he felt the jolt of a lightning bolt cleave the gigantic oak in half. He never heard the crack of thunder that should be associated with a lightning strike, but he did feel and hear the split of the enormous tree and the thud as one half of the trunk fell and shook the soggy ground.

He felt his grip slipping on the upper branch, and he had no feeling in his feet, which were still tingling from the electrical shock of the lightning bolt. But as he released his grip, he didn't fall as expected. Johnny was beside him and holding him on the thin branch. Bird was upwind, using his body to shield Benji from the worst of the wind. Johnny kept saying, "We'll be here, we'll be here…"

CHAPTER FORTY-FIVE

Dawn arrived the following morning. The air was cool, and the sun was bright. For the living, it appeared that God had taken a great eraser to the sky to blot out yesterday's storm. The Triplett family emerged from the church basement, fearful of the upcoming day. James was ferried to the island with EMS and the deputies for a complete search of the island. The first site to search was their home.

The devastation of the island was as complete as the rescuers had feared. Worse storms had been recorded in the past, but that was before the time of this generation. The single paved road that ran the length of the island had been covered with sand, requiring a four-wheel-drive vehicle. At places, the road had been damaged by erosion of the roadbed under the pavement, causing total collapse of the highway. Debris covered the road. As they made their way down the island, they carefully searched the highway and the roadside for signs of life. They encountered occasional scared pets and wildlife, but no signs of people.

The Triplett house was as bad as James had feared, but more importantly, Eddie's truck was overturned in the driveway. No one was in the truck, and the bed apparently had been nearly full of those curious stones, which had spilled over into the sand dune fronting the property. The house was gone. A few of the heavy piling supports remained. They had been cemented deeply into the sand. Nothing else remained.

Behind the house, the great oak tree had split in two. One side lay flat on the ground, and the remaining trunk stood with a noted tilt. At the top of what remained of the tree, the very top, was a body. It looked like…

"Benji! That's my boy Benji up there! My God, get him down. Get him down now!"

The EMTs wasted no time scrambling up the tree to the still body of the teenager. The first one to reach the body yelled down, "There's a pulse! He's opening his eyes!"

Benji was gently lowered to the ground, and lifesaving measures were begun. Oxygen was administered, IV fluids were begun, and a warming blanket was wrapped around him. James sat by his side in the ambulance boat as it powered to the mainland.

Benji occasionally opened his eyes and smiled. He repeated one sentence over and over. "Johnny never left me."

CHAPTER FORTY-SIX

Once again, the Triplett family was camped out in the hospital. Benji's vital signs had stabilized, and he was more alert. The doctors said that he had experienced severe exposure and multiple contusions and bruises. He had several abrasions from the movement of the branches in the fork of the old oak. He had been so tightly wedged in place that the high velocity of the wind had tightened the branches around him, grabbing his flesh. The doctors came by later in the morning and reported that Benji would make a full and hopefully quick recovery. He could even leave that afternoon.

The problem was, the family had no home to go to. Their home had been totally destroyed. But their cousin Mildred once again came to the rescue. She had an uncanny ability of showing up to help exactly when needed and her presence at the hospital was not unexpected. "If you don't mind roughing it for a while, we've got a home over here on the mainland that you could use till your home is rebuilt. I know that Captain Smith will need your help with repairs and reconstruction of Sailor's Rest."

The sheriff had a lot of questions for Benji. For starters, why had he been abducted in the face of a category 4 hurricane? James's questions only started with that. What had happened to Murphy and Eddie? Why had they been so interested in the Triplett home? But those questions could wait till Benji was a bit stronger. There was no certainty that he would even remember the events of the previous evening.

....

James would have been content to stay at Benji's bedside till he was released, but early in the afternoon, he received a call from the sheriff's department, asking him to come over to the site of his house as soon as he could get there. James took J.J. with him since the young boy didn't like hospitals anymore. Once again, they had to traverse a coating of debris and damaged streets to get to their house. Now there was yellow crime-scene tape encircling the property. Of the eight pilings that had supported the house, three were left. Eddie's truck still lay where it had been found earlier in the morning, overturned on the edge of the driveway. As it overturned, it had dumped almost a bed full of Benji's peculiar stones. They had then been held on the ground beneath the inverted bed of the truck.

The sheriff bent down and picked up one of the stones. He rubbed it hard on his pants leg and showed it to James. "What do you make of that?"

"Well, it looks like Benji's lucky stone, but there must be hundreds if not thousands of them."

The sheriff smiled broadly. "Well, I reckon it is right lucky." He pulled out his penknife and pried out the blade. He made a groove in the surface of one of the stones and gave it to James. "Now look at the groove I've made. What do you think?"

"It's yellow. Is that...?"

"Yep, I think that's the real thing. As best I can figure, ol' Murphy figured out that Benji's lucky stone was Spanish gold. He either tricked or fooled that simpleminded Eddie into helping him dig it out of your backyard. He wasn't absolutely sure of the site, so he brought Benji along to point out the right spot. They got a pile of the stones before the storm got them."

After inspection of the concrete slab, James and J.J. walked down the bank toward the sound. The pier was mostly intact. It was missing about half of its boards, but the frame was still there. Some of the old Bankers would later figure that the flooding had

193

occurred so fast that the pier had rapidly been submerged, saving it from the damaging wind. The brush, trees, and ground cover that had carpeted the bank had been stripped as thoroughly as if someone had raked the area clean and handpicked the leaves from the trees.

James's attention was drawn to the big oak tree again. Now half of it was on the ground. The bark had been seared at the site of the split, indicating a lightning strike.

The sheriff walked by and observed, "Man, it's a miracle that Benji survived that. The tip of that top branch was probably the only thing that remained above water in the storm surge."

J.J. was looking at the bottom of the split and talking to himself again. "Okay, I'll look for the shiny things in the wood." J.J. looked up at James. "Johnny wants you to look at the bottom of the tree."

James was about to apologize to the sheriff for J.J.'s interruption, but in view of recent events, he had learned to heed any communication from Johnny. He and the sheriff stooped down to look at the smoking cleft of the tree.

The sheriff observed, "There's something grown into the tree. It looks like an old sea chest or strongbox. It's a little bigger than a shoebox, and it's grown into the wood like it's part of the tree. See the metal fittings? They're hardly rusted. I guess they were protected after the tree grew around them.

"You know, James, you've got a fortune from the bed of that pickup, and I'm seeing bunches more of those stones or coins or whatever under that fallen side of the tree. I'll bet there is something valuable inside that chest that someone hid under this tree a long time ago."

James was so stunned that he was absolutely speechless. But he thought he knew who had hidden all that treasure.

....

The site was secured and guarded by a combination of sheriff's deputies and local volunteer firefighters until the state government was able to do an official visit to the site.

194

The stones were found to be Spanish coins of precious metal and were believed to have originated from a Spanish treasure ship. More coins were found at the site, along with a second chest. The second chest had weathered the centuries better and was almost intact. Even more interesting was the small chest that had become encased in the ancient oak tree. The remaining half of the old oak tree was cut down, and the section containing the chest was moved to a secure location. The chest was dismembered and found to be loaded with precious stones. They were all of the finest quality and could not even be valued— given their base value and the circumstances of their discovery, they were priceless.

As usual, the government swooped in, and the tax assessors and then the lawyers all had opinions on what to do with the treasure. James had hired his own lawyers as well. Finally, a solution was reached that satisfied the historians, the tax assessors, the many government officials, and most importantly, the Tripletts, who would now be able to put money into a house, raise their children more comfortably than they had felt they ever could, and fund their education. They also gave back to the community by funding an endowment so that the Bankers could recover from the hurricane and be enriched for generations to come.

The riches from the treasure were so immense that the Tripletts could not even imagine how to spend a fraction of their bounty. A sizable part would end up loaned or given to museums, and Sailor's Rest would have its endowment enlarged. But still, the bulk of the treasure remained.

....

One year later, the Tripletts had survived both a hurricane and a subsequent whirlwind of activity. The injection of resources into Triplett's Cove had ensured a never-ending torrent of construction activity. As the anniversary of the hurricane approached, James and his family decided to host a celebration for the entire village. *Rucker John's* was an accommodating

195

restaurant in a nearby community that was willing and able to host the entire community of Triplett's Cove for an evening. The entire population of one hundred accepted the invitation for the meal and celebration.

After the meal, James stood and clinked his glass to get everyone's attention. "I'd like to thank you for coming for the anniversary of the big blow. You know, last year we were at a pretty low point when we moved to Grandpa's little house. I guess we had forgotten what community and family mean in Triplett's Cove. Your caring and generous acts meant so much to us from the time we moved to the Banks.

Now the treasure we discovered—I should say Benji and J.J. discovered—has been catalogued and suitably sent to the appropriate agencies. What we didn't know right away was that Benji and Kelsey had already been impressed by the beauty and novelty of those lucky stones. Days before the storm hit, they removed hundreds of the stones and hid them in the floor of our old Suburban."

James took a deep breath and looked a bit sheepish as he admitted, "In all the excitement and activity, they were overlooked. I've talked with our lawyers, and they are of the opinion that since those stones were discovered and removed before there was knowledge of the treasure or a discovery of what these stones were, they might be excluded from the taxes imposed on the treasure. The legal folks were puzzled about just what to do with these objects. I intend to give that problem to you." James was careful not to say that the objects were precious metals.

James raised his glass as a signal, and the three Triplett children emerged from the kitchen area, pulling a large red Radio Flyer wagon loaded with three bulging burlap bags. Inside the three bags were smaller bags labeled with the names of every Triplett Cove family in attendance and tags that said "lucky stones."

CHAPTER FORTY-SEVEN

In future years, the Triplett children will leave home, complete their educations, and begin their own families. They will pursue careers and lives away from the barrier islands, but they will always return. They will return not only for the usual reason of vacations, but also to bathe in the culture of the plainspoken and honest Bankers. They will return to nourish their souls.

The grown Triplett children will share a bond. Ever since the time of the great storm, they will, at times, feel a presence. The presence will be a source of calm and a source of strength that they can always draw on when they feel as though they have gone past their limits.

The presence will have the voice of a child, Johnny. He may be heard saying, "Don't you be afraid. Johnny's not afraid." Sometimes the presence may say, "Climb higher; me and Bird got you." Or sometimes, "We've got you. Me and Bird are here for you." Are they haunted? Perhaps it is a haunting or a possession. But maybe it is more the comforting presence of an old spirit.

In Triplett's Cove, stories will continue to circulate regarding the great storm and the miraculous survival of Benjamin Triplett in the face of a severe hurricane and criminality.

Still, in the evenings when the breezes rustle the treetops, Bankers will listen for the gentle voice of the little boy, the flapping of a parrot's wings, and a faint whistled tune.

RESOURCES

My idea for *Boy in the Treetops* originated years ago on a plantation tour of Carter's Grove Plantation on the James River in Virginia. As the story percolated in my mind over the years, I had opportunities to tour other plantations or plantation sites to absorb more stories.

Such sites included Brookgreen Gardens in Murrell's Inlet, South Carolina, which is now a famous sculpture garden but that is built on the site of four rice plantations. Guided tours give the story of the labors of enslaved people who produced the rice and built the rice empire of the south.

The Hopsowee Plantation in Georgetown, South Carolina, is the ancestral home of the Lynch family of founding fathers. The plantation house is now a private residence that graciously allows tours. Video presentations give enormous insight into the lives of the enslaved population.

The Hampton Plantation in McClellanville, South Carolina, is now a state park and an active site of research into plantation life. The knowledgeable staff was helpful and patient in answering questions.

Further knowledge of the lives of enslaved people comes from none other than Franklin Delano Roosevelt. In the midst of the Great Depression, one of the hardest-hit segments of society was writers. FDR enlisted writers in the Federal Writer's Project, from 1936 to 1938, under the auspices of the WPA. Writers were sent across the south to interview people over eighty years of age who had been enslaved, to get firsthand accounts of life during slavery before those stories were lost forever. Part of that narrative is included in the publication *North Carolina Slave Narratives*. That project has been valuable in providing a picture of the day-to-day lives of people who were enslaved.

A further look at life during enslavement and the Gullah culture on the rice plantation system is found in *The Water Brought Us* by Muriel Miller Branch, published in 1995.

Parts of the life at sea depicted in this book, including a look at the gun deck, were inspired by a Victor Hugo novel, *Ninety-Three*. One chapter, "The Battle with the Cannon," describes the havoc that can occur as a result of a moment of inattention on the gun deck.

Legends and myths about the Outer Banks abound. Many of us have heard these stories and visited these sites since childhood. One resource I have used is *Graveyard of the Atlantic: Shipwrecks of the North Carolina Coast* by David Stick, first published in 1952.

The Graveyard of the Atlantic Museum in Hatteras, North Carolina documents the hazards of the dangerous coast along the barrier islands and does have a reproduction of the Theodosia Burr Alston portrait mentioned in this book.

There is a long-term care facility in the area with origins similar to the facility I created for my story. I've toured that facility and found it to be among the finest homes for the aging I have encountered. I've used some artistic license to create my fictional facility, Sailor's Rest, and the village of Triplett's Cove. The staff and residents of my fictional facility are also born of my imagination and my forty years spent caring for patients in long-term care. Unfortunately, the inspiration for *Sailor's Rest* in my story was damaged by hurricane Florence. It was beginning to recover when it took a second hit from hurricane Dorian. It has since closed.

Finally, Chapter 18 of *Boy in the Treetops* was the basis of a short story written for Reedsy.com in response to a request for stories inspired by their prompt. *Location, location* in September 2020.

ABOUT THE AUTHOR

Dr. Sam Newsome, a family doctor, lives in King North Carolina.

Dr. Newsome's first novel, *Jackie*, explores the miraculous life of a disadvantaged youth diagnosed with the autism spectrum who is destined for heroism. *Jackie* received the Garcia Memorial Award from Reader Views for the best fiction of 2015.

His next novel, *Joe Peas*, explored the quests of the title character and his local doctor to remain individuals in a world that increasingly rewards conformity. The book celebrates family, friendship, faith, and healing. It also gave Dr. Newsome an opportunity to entertain and educate his readers about long-term care and good health habits. *Joe Peas* was awarded a first place in fiction by the Colorado Independent Publishers Association in 2017.

Dr. Newsome's current story combines the unique culture of the Bankers with the myths, legends, the unique history of the region and a host of colorful characters. He hopes that readers will enjoy the story as much as he enjoyed creating it.